THE
DUNNING-
KRUGER
EFFECT

THE
DUNNING-KRUGER EFFECT

A NOVEL

ANDRÉS STOOPENDAAL

Translated by Alex Fleming

ATRIA BOOKS

New York   London   Toronto   Sydney   New Delhi

ATRIA
BOOKS

An Imprint of Simon & Schuster, LLC
1230 Avenue of the Americas
New York, NY 10020

First Atria Books hardcover edition June 2024

ATRIA BOOKS and colophon are trademarks of Simon & Schuster, LLC

Simon & Schuster: Celebrating 100 Years of Publishing in 2024

For information about special discounts for bulk purchases, please
contact Simon & Schuster Special Sales at 1-866-506-1949 or
business@simonandschuster.com.

The Simon & Schuster Speakers Bureau can bring authors to your live event. For
more information or to book an event, contact the Simon & Schuster Speakers
Bureau at 1-866-248-3049 or visit our website at www.simonspeakers.com.

Interior design by Jill Putorti

Manufactured in the United States of America

1 3 5 7 9 10 8 6 4 2

Library of Congress Cataloging-in-Publication Data is available.

ISBN 978-1-6680-2019-7
ISBN 978-1-6680-2021-0 (ebook)

THE
DUNNING-
KRUGER
EFFECT

1

FRODO'S DISAPPEARANCE

It was only in late March 2018, as fate would have it just weeks after the publication of Carl Cederström's peculiar article in *Svenska Dagbladet* about Jordan B. Peterson's *12 Rules for Life: An Antidote to Chaos*,[*] that I seriously came to understand what a truly incendiary, if not scandalous, figure the Canadian psychologist cut, among not only ordinary folk but also people in my own social circle.

My girlfriend, Maria, who was by this point fairly instrumental in managing my social life, and at whose place I was increasingly spending the night, had decided to invite her friend

---

[*] *12 Rules* would be published in Swedish translation only later that year, by Mondial.

Agnes, a PhD student in art history, and Agnes's partner, Otto, a historian of ideas, over for dinner one Friday evening at her apartment on Linnégatan in Gothenburg.

Otto was a few years past thirty, as was I, and Agnes a few below, like Maria. Maria was a pretty good cook (we were both big fans of Anthony Bourdain[*]) and had prepared a lamb casserole that had had to spend most of the afternoon on the stove.

She had warned me, though.

It would be a good idea to tread softly, so to speak, with Agnes and Otto (and be a little extra nice to them), since just a few weeks earlier their cat, Frodo—so named after the hero in *The Lord of the Rings*—had fallen from their third-floor window and subsequently vanished without a trace. One of them, either Agnes or Otto, had forgotten to shut the kitchen window. They had found claw marks on the window ledge, Maria told us. Poor Frodo, a rather diminutive cat, must have been—or at least so I imagined as Maria recounted the story—nonchalantly sniffing around by the window, surveying the street outside, when all of a sudden he lost his balance; in full-blown panic he would have scrabbled at the window ledge, only to slowly but surely— and possibly to the screech of splayed claws on metal (like in a *Tom & Jerry* cartoon)—lose his grip completely, at which time he must have plunged headlong in the darkness and cold and down onto the pavement, where he, Frodo, this patently indoor

---

[*]At the time still living. Bourdain would be found dead by suicide on June 8, 2018, in his room at Le Chambard Hotel in Kaysersberg, Alsace.

cat, hella terrified by the wider world, would presumably have perished. Agnes and Otto hadn't given up hope, mind; they had plastered half of Kungsladugård and Majorna with posters of little Frodo. Beneath a photo of the timid cat, the whole sorry tale was described. The infuriatingly unshut window. The claw marks on the window ledge. Frodo's putative nosedive onto the hard tarmac below.

So, Frodo had already been gone a few weeks, and, according to Maria, who knew Agnes well, it was clear that they had started to lose hope just a tad. Maria told me she had heard it in Agnes's voice when they had last chatted. Notwithstanding all that, I'd venture to say that spirits at dinner were high. Maria and Agnes mostly reminisced about their student days in Lund, and there was only the odd mention of Frodo. Like when Agnes talked about how much she missed the little cat, while Otto caressed her back with a very serious and strained expression, torn between the urge to comfort Agnes and to scrutinize our reactions; as though Otto, model boyfriend that he was, nevertheless to some extent presumed that I, mainly—at whom he cast a suspicious glance when Agnes was perilously close to tears—actually found the whole story, and, indeed, this whole pet fixation, pretty ridiculous, which was basically true. It was awkward. Agnes valiantly squeezed her boyfriend's hand. They would get through this *together*. "Yes, yes, we will, Agnes. We *will* get through this."

It seemed obvious to me that Frodo—about whom my thoughts were already in the *past tense*, as *ex-Frodo*, say—had been something of a "transitional object" for the couple, even if they themselves were naturally incapable of regarding him as such. If Agnes and Otto managed to look after a little cat and were both capable of showing him the requisite tenderness and consideration, thus proving to each other their "adult responsibility" as well as warm feelings for the cute little furball, they could then "level up," as it were, and perhaps eventually allow themselves to make a *real little baby*, an undertaking that would reasonably demand both responsibility and maturity.

That Frodo had fallen from the window had, I assumed, not only come as a shock to them both; it was, conceivably, a genuine disaster. They probably wouldn't say as much openly to each other, but I imagined the issue hovering over them all the same: *What if that had happened to a real little baby?* The fact of the matter was that such terrible tragedies did occur at times. Every now and then kids did fall from windows, much to society's horror—and *that* was certainly no laughing matter.

Truth be told, I myself shuddered slightly at the thought of something like that happening to Maria and me, even though we didn't yet have kids of our own (and perhaps never would). Admittedly, we did have—or, rather, Maria had—Molly. But the thought of that little white Pomeranian having the audacity to fall from a window felt far too outlandish for me to take seriously.

Agnes also revealed that they had just put up another set of fliers on their block, Poster 2.0, with the headline: *Frodo is still missing!* So eager was she for us to see it that she whipped out her smartphone and started scrolling through her photos. In the photo on the (ambitiously) laminated, and thereby waterproof, poster, there was an additional picture of Frodo, this time in color, which made the little cat's unique coat patterns clearer, all to facilitate a correct identification. As I gazed at the image, I strangely enough felt a keen impulse to pretend I'd seen Frodo near my flat in Majorna, but I bit my tongue, tried to rustle up a look of sincere concern, and hoped that it would seem like my heart was bleeding for them, so to speak.

Agnes was, I noted, very keen to emphasize that Frodo was *their* cat. Agnes's *and* Otto's. They were in this *together*. On the poster they had given both of their phone numbers. Just in case, I guess. So two numbers. And two email addresses. Yes, I could unequivocally state that they were both indeed traumatized—and at the same time strangely bound—by the tragedy of Frodo's disappearance.

After dinner we retired to the living room, where Maria and Agnes went on drinking white, while I took another Urquel and Otto a bottle of Stigbergets pilsner from a local brewery. It was only then that the generally breezy atmosphere would take an abrupt turn. It had all started with a pretty uncontroversial conversation about Sweden's "consensus culture," and the conformism that could be deemed characteristic of Scandinavian countries. We unanimously agreed to leave unsaid for the moment whether said conformism and consensus culture were for better or for worse. In this respect we were still pretty much of one mind, as we had been about most of what was discussed at dinner. Donald Trump was *dumb*. Putin was *dumb*. Margaret Thatcher had, admittedly, been Europe's (and maybe even the world's) first female prime minister, and as such perhaps deserved just a smidgen of feminist admiration—not to mention the fact that she'd spoken out against climate change at a relatively early stage—but in the grand scheme of things she, too, had been *dumb*. A great many people were generally *dumb*—on that we were all agreed—perhaps especially so in those days.

Thus, with no great friction, we could all agree on the existence of what might be termed a Swedish consensus culture (without ipso facto outing ourselves as exponents of that social norm). Otto soon got onto the 1938 Saltsjöbaden Agreement between the trade unions and employer associations, and the Swedish labor movement's long and well-documented collaboration with industry, which had largely, he believed, been a boon for Sweden. A statement that was music to my ears, and perhaps lulled me into a false sense of security, for it was then that I thought—since Otto seemed like a "sensible" chap with a certain understanding of social democracy's reformist strategy—that the time was ripe for me to recount a Jordan B. Peterson anecdote that my friend Johannes had told me during a session at Plankan, our local watering hole.

The anecdote was about an elderly Canadian man who stops at a pedestrian crossing to wait for the light to turn green. It's early in the morning and freezing cold; maybe minus 4. No car as far as the eye can see. The city is empty, deserted. Still, the man stands there waiting for ages—*a long, long time*—for the light to go from red to green. For this Canadian pedestrian, to cross on red would be simply unthinkable. It makes no difference that the traffic is pretty much nonexistent, or that he, this lone pedestrian, is in actual fact the only traffic there is! He abides by the law and the rules, he does, for that's what he has always done. Now, if one were to apply the terms of personality psychology to this man, one would say that he has a strong measure of agreeableness and is also, I assumed, a relatively conscientious person; in this case extreme in his exactitude and complete symbiosis with Canadian society's wholly rational (and potentially universally applicable) traffic rules. Which I supposed was perhaps why Peterson had used the man as an example of something that to me seemed equally characteristic of many of us Nordic peoples: an almost idiotic readiness to comply with law and order.

"Not that there's necessarily anything wrong with that, generally speaking," I said. "But then again it might not be wholly positive. The man undeniably stands there freezing like a poor animal, without needing to!"

Otto replied with grim resolve that there may be some degree of truth to that, certainly, but then he added, surprisingly harshly, and so out of the blue that I almost recoiled, that he actually thought Peterson was "a joke," and that he couldn't understand how anyone could take the man seriously. It was as though he hadn't even listened to my (or, rather, Peterson's) example of our interesting Nordic psychology. For my part, while recounting the anecdote, I hadn't quite picked up on his apparent transformation into a completely different—all but *crackling*—person.

For a second I thought Otto was on the brink of tears. I also got the unpleasant feeling that he could easily throw a punch or something. The thing is, even though I'd bumped into Agnes and Otto a few times in town, I didn't really know Otto; to me he was a blank page. Maria and Agnes said nothing, but Maria shot me a glance that I interpreted as an expression of surprise and perhaps an appeal for caution. To my knowledge she wasn't really up on who Peterson was, and in a way neither was I. Agnes, for her part, looked altogether unfussed.

Though I soon suspected that Otto had some sort of *beef* with Peterson, under the circumstances it didn't feel right to completely capitulate, so to say. As such, it seemed a not-entirely-inappropriate moment to bring up Carl Cederström's bizarre *Svenska Dagbladet* article, in which Cederström, an associate professor in organization studies, described the psychologist as someone who looked up to or even praised bullies and scorned the weak. The article was illustrated with an image of Nelson Muntz from *The Simpsons*; a classic problem child in the cartoon who, as Peterson would have it, serves as a corrective for keeping weak and pathetic behaviors in check.

"Personally, I have a hard time—a really hard time, frankly..." I said, "believing that Peterson actually looks up to bullies and scorns the weak." I went on: "Though I haven't read *12 Rules for Life* myself."

"Yes, but why *would* anyone read it!" Otto bristled. Something I chose to ignore.

"But wasn't Cederström's article extremely black-and-white and weird? Was he not guilty of guilt by association? A clear-cut case of bias, surely? I mean, he went on to mention Breivik, the alt-right, the far right, Trump, and the like. *Only 'lost boys' admire Peterson*, yada yada yada. The only one missing was Hitler!"

"Apparently young men call him and *cry* down the line," Otto said jeeringly.

"Even Peterson cries sometimes—on his own YouTube channel!" Agnes jumped in merrily; she didn't seem at all as outraged by the Canadian psychologist as her partner, for whom the man was clearly an extreme *trigger*.

"Well, I for one have no intention of reading him," Otto declared sourly. "He has no *substance!*" he went on. "There are loads of contemporary conservative thinkers who are better. Way more worth reading. If I had to read conservative thinkers today I'd prefer . . . well, maybe Mark Steyn or Peter Hitchens. Peterson pretends he's some kind of expert on myths and folktales, but he takes examples from works that he clearly doesn't realize were originally written by Hans Christian Andersen. . . . You know, it actually *upsets* me to talk about him. I mean, he isn't good! What sort of people like that person? *Well, actually I do know . . . what they are.*"

Otto, the historian of ideas, had more or less hissed that last sentence, and it had also sounded more or less insinuating, as though there was an underlying accusation there. But I couldn't quite make out if it was directed at me, or he'd simply disappeared into some sort of private sphere of festering conflicts and traumas. Perhaps he had a junkie brother who loved Peterson, somehow, and perhaps this (in Otto's eyes) loathsome adoration simply constituted yet another alienating element in their relationship. But it would be extraordinary, if not completely absurd, for him to think *I* belonged to some Swedish alt-right faction or the like. For my political leaning was definitely no secret. I had always been left wing. Much like Otto himself, I assumed, even if he was perhaps to the left of the left on the political spectrum.

In any case, it was clear to me—and I assume the others, too—that Otto's entire bearing had changed. He looked almost emasculated. Sat there with his shoulders hunched, as though preparing to fend off an attack. His gaze had darkened, his eyes anxious and glassy. For a second I pictured Frodo the missing cat and the Canadian psychologist both materializing in the middle of the room, and the latter—the, in Otto's view, would-be deranged and fascistoid right-winger—screaming and blustering at the little cat and transitional object: *You are small and weak, Frodo! You don't even deserve to live!* But the little cat (and baby substitute) didn't deserve Peterson's unreserved taunts. Of course not! Otto's fists may well have been clenched beneath the low coffee table where they were hidden, and his knuckles may well have been turning white, but still he didn't straighten his back. The damage was done. He would not recover.

A man (like Peterson), that intellectual scum, I imagined Otto thinking, a man who was clearly willing to rape and pillage his way through the entire Shire—the hobbit Arcadia—was no better than Saruman himself! In that moment it didn't seem at all inconceivable that that was exactly how Otto saw things. He had *lost it*, in short, and in almost exactly the same way that associate professor Cederström had *lost it* in his bizarre article in *Svenskan*. Both had seemed in thrall to passions; *pathos* had occupied the place that had once housed their identities; their personalities had completely dissolved; their autonomy dissipated. They had allowed themselves to be hurled into chaos— and *ressentiment*.

"I just don't get how anyone can take him seriously," Otto grumbled, appearing all of a sudden both highly hot and bothered and pathetic all at once, to the point of deep despondency. It was a very strange scene to behold—and from what I could tell the man wasn't even all that drunk!

"I just don't get why people take Peterson seriously," he repeated. "How can anyone take such a character seriously?"

"Still, it seems like a whole lot of people in the world *do* take him seriously. And he clearly provokes a lot of people, too. In any case, Camille Paglia has called him the greatest Canadian thinker since Marshall McLuhan."

"But isn't Paglia mainly just a provocateur?" Agnes wondered.

"Possibly," I said, "but she's also a pretty brilliant person."

Nope, when it came to Paglia I had no plans of backing down an inch. I liked her keenly.

"I would even go so far as to say that she has certain . . . well, wholly genius aspects . . ." I went on. "Which for that matter I *don't* think Peterson has."

I'd thrown in that last part mainly to please or even appease Otto, who for at least a second lit up with what I assumed were gratitude and relief; but no, I didn't think Professor Peterson was a genius, absolutely not. Professor Paglia, on the other hand, had been an idol of mine for years, even if lately—that is, in the late 2010s—I'd been increasingly disappointed by the author of the monumental *Sexual Personae*.

One of her more recent books, *Glittering Images*, which discussed Western art—from Nefertiti's grave to George Lucas's volcano-planet duel in *Revenge of the Sith*—hadn't lived up to my expectations. Besides which, she'd clearly gotten ever more stuck in the role of someone who both wrote and spoke in what she herself termed "sound bites."

She doesn't really get to the heart of it, I thought and took a swig of my Urquel, supposing it would be a faux pas to air some of her more famous quotes, such as: "There is no female Mozart because there is no female Jack the Ripper." Personally, I assumed Paglia was right on that one—since there was de facto no female counterpart to the musical genius of Mozart or Beethoven or Bach (which was kind of sad in a way), and there was de facto no female counterpart to serial killers like

Jack the Ripper or Ted Bundy or Jeffrey Dahmer (and a good thing, too!)—but it could take all night to explain why. And it definitely wouldn't be worth it.

Maria and Agnes had gradually—and perhaps more or less demonstratively—started to turn to each other to discuss other things entirely, as though signaling that it was time for us men to amuse ourselves for a while. It didn't seem unlikely that they were mildly embarrassed by Otto's exaggeratedly emotional reaction. But then again they might not have been all that interested in the topic, either. It wasn't like they were Peterson's target market, exactly. Or at least not in the same way that Otto and I were.

Neither he nor I, it has to be said, were actually confused or lost young men—or at least not in our own eyes, I guess—but men we were, and we were also at least to some degree involved—Otto more so than myself—in the fields of academia that Peterson considered his targets.

As I would only later come to understand, Peterson saw Marxist, postmodern, and above all feminist-oriented academics—and institutions—as his *enemies*. In essence, he wanted to close down all the humanities and rebuild them from the ground up, since the world of academia was corrupt beyond redemption. For decades, professors had increasingly become the activist defenders of political correctness and identity politics. But the revolution ate its own children; with time the ideology that they had championed would consume itself. The universities had, in addition, been *feminized*, according to Peterson; the prestige of having an academic (humanities) background was constantly being devalued. The Canadian psychologist regarded political correctness as an umbrella term for everything that had been *de rigueur* in academia of late: gender studies, women's studies, postcolonial studies, intersectionality; so-called whiteness studies.

Now, if Otto identified with Marxism, postmodernism, and feminism—if these were an integral aspect of his academic persona and identity (and, perhaps, his strategy for winning over his peers)—then it possibly wasn't so strange that he would react as strongly as he did. But the fact that Peterson could seem so monstrous in Otto's eyes was, at the time, simply astonishing to me, even if I should, admittedly, have suspected that Cederström's article would be symptomatic—a sort of *morphological paradigm*—of how many people nevertheless viewed the Canadian psychologist.

Anyhow, I tried to coax Otto into small talk about other things, and after a while the reluctant guest started to tell me about an essay he was working on—I seem to recall it was on the concept of the deep state—but in the wake of the Peterson Debate, any good-mannered banter was well and truly off the table. The atmosphere was irreparably damaged. Peterson had exposed something. A wound? A sore point? Otto's contention that Peterson was "a joke" was hardly a real argument in my view. On the one hand, that there were contemporary conservative thinkers who were more worth reading seemed plausible enough—that much I could buy (clueless as I was when it came to conservative thinkers); on the other hand, Otto hadn't really put his finger on what was so conservative about Peterson's thinking in the first place.

As for me, I still didn't get what this thinking was, and I certainly didn't get what about it more or less whipped people like Otto and Cederström up into hysterics when confronted with it. Be that as it may, that I would sooner or later have to read Peterson's book and make the effort to familiarize myself with his thinking was now seeming increasingly unavoidable.

Once Agnes and Otto had finally left—much earlier than expected (we never got round to playing Trivial Pursuit, which I'd kind of been looking forward to)—both Maria and I breathed a sigh of relief. As I got down to the dishes I had a certain trepidation that Maria would blame me for sabotaging the agreeable vibe, but thankfully she, too, expressed shock at how "weird" Otto had gotten at the mere mention of Peterson's name. Something that she linked to the "trauma" of Frodo's disappearance. But it wasn't like I'd been particularly offensive or unruly in any way. I had led the conversation, as I myself and Maria also saw it, with a demonstratively reasoned, formal tone, which I suppose may in and of itself have provoked the historian of ideas. Nor had I defended Peterson to any great degree. I was also grateful that Agnes hadn't assumed an overly loyal and uncompromising defensive position vis-à-vis her partner. It would have been sad if Agnes had started to think badly of me, especially seeing as she often dropped in at Maria's or popped by to join us when we were out in cafés, and so on.

As such, I would be seeing Agnes more than Otto going forward—provided, of course, that my relationship with Maria was to last, which, given that we'd already been together a year and a half, felt extremely feasible.

Fact was, we were very happy together. We had what one would call a "serious" relationship. We also had a number of shared interests. Maria had initially studied art history, but she had changed tack and was now reading librarianship over in Borås, where she had one year left of her training. She was cute, pretty smart, and exciting in erotic respects. Sometimes she would surprise even me by going along with things that I think are difficult or possibly compromising to consciously articulate, even if just to yourself. So long as we were singing from the same song sheet, as it were, and she got what I would term "the concept"—which she seemed to do intuitively, in fact—she was never disgusted or in any way alarmed by the "acts," "scenarios," or even "episodes" that occasionally popped up in and of themselves. I'm not sure even I knew where some of them came from.

Now, admittedly we were just two people, but even so I would sometimes find myself thinking of our lovemaking—in group-dynamic terms—as a sort of erotic *play community* whose diffuse rules emerged—there and then—from an exclusive, chaotic, and unique *play sphere*. In such a way one could draw parallels between the mystical rules of said *play sphere* and the so-called willing suspension of disbelief in the reading of literary works. Only if disbelief surfaced—if the fiction didn't work—would love's spell, or what one could perhaps also call that of *the sexual manuscript*, be broken. It would backfire, just as art backfired when said suspension was not achieved.

Sometimes I would even find myself contemplating the German-American psychologist Kurt Lewin's behavior equation, as described in his 1936 work *Principles of Topological Psychology*. The equation, $B = f(P, E)$, describes behavior (B) as a function (f) of the person (P) and his or her environment (E). This equation was usually paired with Lewin's field theory, which posits that an individual's "life space" comprises a psychological field that includes both the individual and their immediate environment. As such, an individual's actions can't be explained—or at all understood—by internal or external factors alone but are rather the product of a complex interplay of internal and external motivations.

A group—or perhaps even just *a couple* (like Maria and myself)—thus always consisted of more than the sum of its individual contracting parties. When the group—or in this case *the couple*, or participants in the binary *play sphere*—was formed, it constituted a unified system with *supervening qualities* that would be impossible to understand through an individual evaluation of its parts alone.

Apparently it was my turn to take Molly out that night. I don't know how Maria came to that conclusion, but it didn't really matter anyway. Besides, I could see that her greatest wish was simply to curl up in bed with Grace Coddington's *Grace: A Memoir* and get swept up in its glamorous world. She had gone all in with that book lately. Whenever Maria was reading she was impossible to reach. The strange thing was, she read so slowly that I almost got the feeling she was pretending. It wasn't that she was bad at English. She just read extremely slowly. Yes, even in Swedish. Ah well.

I stopped dead in my tracks in the hallway, Molly's lead dangling from my hand, caught by my own reflection in the full-length mirror. I didn't have any particularly big mirrors at my place, so I found it a little disconcerting to see myself in my own magnificent totality, as it were. No, to be honest it was more that I was genuinely taken aback by how enormously critical I was about my own appearance. Or, more precisely: on that particular night I was surprised by how extremely alien I looked to myself. Namely, I was struck by the fact that my once-so-slender build was starting to exhibit a meatiness that I had never really noticed in myself before. I pinched the layer of subcutaneous fat on my belly and noted that it was still no thicker than one (1) inch (2.54 cm). "Pinch an inch," as an American woman had said to me once in Berlin. Yeah, I'd fancied her all right. According to her, one inch of subcutaneous fat was a sign of good health.

It struck me now that I not only *was*, but was increasingly starting to *look like*, a grown man. My waist wasn't as slim as before, and if I didn't consciously suck in my belly and stand up straight it was there; not so big, perhaps, but still. Suddenly I recalled the impression that actor Harvey Keitel had made on me when I saw Jane Campion's *The Piano* for the first time. I'd been in my early teens, maybe, or thereabouts. There had been something hypnotic about that fifty-odd-year-old man's aging, yet muscular, slightly squat and solid physiognomy. Now, it would be unreasonable to claim I felt an erotically tinged attraction to that actor's physique, if that's what you're thinking, but there was absolutely *something* there. An intense fascination—and perhaps a kind of envy. A longing for a body with weight, strength, and power. After all, I was just a scrawny kid when I saw the film; perhaps back then I didn't even feel like I had a body. In any case not a body with strength and power, and certainly not weight. I'd thought: *Well, my movements may well be nimble, like an elf's—but at the end of the day an elf is, by its very elfishness, so to speak,* masculinity's antithesis. *An elf is an* androgynous being. Its slender, sexless body could never be a source of masculine pride.

Well, long gone were the days when I could still catch an air of elfishness in my look. If I'm honest, all things aside, this realization filled me with a sort of happiness. (Though to be fair I was pleasantly intoxicated by this point.) I *looked* older and I *was* older—and this didn't really bother me at all (even though I couldn't deny that the man now gazing back at me was something of a stranger to himself). It would be extremely narcissistic to feel wronged by the passage of time—though surely wronged wasn't how I felt, was it? Was it not rather gratitude

I felt—yes, actual genuine gratitude—that time had shaped me into a person—at least outwardly—who was perhaps better able to shoulder certain types of responsibility in life? Indeed, perhaps even the sort of "adult responsibility" that I had (not unmockingly) inferred Agnes and Otto were doing their utmost to summon, through their project (or experiment) with the now-missing cat Frodo?

Earlier on in the day, I remembered, Maria had brought up the topic of kids in a way that wasn't quite a request, but wasn't entirely without its pretensions, either. We'd been together so long that it was a given that the question would come up sooner or later. While the topic had in fact filled me with sadness, I was pleased that my comments, at least as I saw it, had made me come across as a relatively wise individual. Indeed, when is one really ready for parenthood? No one knows. I'd said: *Perhaps no one's ever ready?* Now, later, as I stood before my own reflection, I concluded that at the very least it was unquestionably a plus to be able to take care of oneself. Of someone else. I cast a glance at Molly, who was quivering with anticipation ahead of her short walk. "All right, all right, I'll get my coat."

It felt objectionable to imagine Molly as some sort of baby surrogate or biological Tamagotchi, but I couldn't deny that at dinner I'd also toyed with the idea that perhaps she, too, was a kind of "transitional object" for Maria and me, in the same way that I'd seen Frodo as one for Agnes and Otto.

A kind of experiment. Yes, I'd thought I'd sounded wise during that kids chat, but now I realized that my words could just as easily have seemed like muddled clichés. *The child is father of the man*, I'd said. Maria had asked me to repeat that possibly age-old saying, and I'd changed the gender: *The child is mother of the woman*. Maria had contemplated these words in silence for a while. *She should get this*, I thought. *She's pretty smart and all*. But I also realized that the initial breeziness or perhaps *impartiality* with which we'd embarked upon this most sensitive topic wasn't all that compatible with such an existential and almost solemn statement.

Hypothetically speaking, any notional babymaking lay some way down the line, at least. Maria would have to finish her studies. Maybe get a job somewhere. But anyway, I felt no acute concern on that front. In days gone by I might have pondered the risk that I was way too damaged by my troubled upbringing to be a good father, but perhaps I'd been too hard on myself. Maria was great. Her family were super bougie, but great all the same; they had, at the very least, produced her, her *genius*— I was almost tempted to say. Put it this way: If Maria was to fall pregnant, I wouldn't cry tears of blood. The opposite, in fact! We would handle the situation when or if it should arise. That it would then entail a lifelong commitment and *extreme* curtailment of my personal freedoms was terrifying. Freedom as I knew it would be over. But had I not started to tire of that same freedom? For many years I had had no responsibility for anyone but myself. At the same time, I couldn't help but admit that I'd repeatedly failed to take that responsibility. Informally, I still saw myself as a "goof-off." Someone who did *fuckups*.

Though, it was true, in recent years I had matured slightly; I'd toed the line.

And now the domain of my responsibility had also expanded to encompass both Maria and her dog, Molly, and there was something beautiful (almost touching) and natural about that. The mere act of taking that little creature for a walk was to take adult responsibility. My responsibility for Maria was different, I expect. Yes, that was probably true. I had no responsibility for her per se. Obviously. It was more like I was *accountable to her*, in a quasi-juridical sense, as though to a judge or supplementary superego.

But if a man were to suddenly attack her? Of course then I would be compelled to defend her, purely physically. Naturally! In essence it was perhaps more about care than responsibility, I thought, and perhaps that was how it was for Maria, too. Those caring or nurturing traits that she had most certainly extended toward me because she felt, I supposed, and perhaps to a much greater degree than I did, that her self-care comprised my person, too.

If we were to ever have kids, I thought, as I clipped the lead onto Molly's bright-pink collar with a certain sense of routine, *that care would in all likelihood be more or less completely redirected toward them*. This was all natural enough in itself, but it could also lead to discord. If in that situation I couldn't bring myself to be mature enough, indeed, *authentically adult* as it were; if I hadn't completely rooted myself in my adulthood, the situation would prove unbearable—and a separation inevitable. Maria's body and soul would belong to another being entirely. My own offspring. Her entire existence would be symbiotically linked to that little individual.

Not that that that would be strange, I thought and suddenly lurched slightly, nothing strange at all, really, it would simply demand *a higher amplitude of adulthood* on my part!

I, too, would have to "level up," and preferably sooner rather than later, given that Maria's longing for babies was—I suspected—programmed into every cell of her slender body, in roughly the same way that it was programmed into Molly's, since Molly was a bitch.

2

THE MOLLY JOKE

Despite the fact that over two months had passed since my eyes had well and truly been opened to how controversial Professor Jordan B. Peterson was to a surprising number of people, including those in my own social circle, on that almost shockingly beautiful May morning—when at breakfast Maria would do the gag involving Molly (or the "Molly Joke" or the "Molly Schtick" as I also called it) for the last time—I still hadn't gotten down to reading the Canadian psychologist's book *12 Rules*.

This wasn't so much a question of oversight on my part, not at all; I simply hadn't had time; in those days my work—or day job—as an administrator for the County Administrative Board's unit for civil protection and emergency preparedness was taking up a considerable amount of my time, even though for the last six months it had only been part-time. Still, I had made an effort to find out more about Peterson, which included listening to *The Joe Rogan Experience* podcast (episodes #877 and #1006) and reading Peterson's Wikipedia page. As such, I had by now learned that Peterson had first come into the public eye at some point in September 2016, after refusing to use gender-neutral pronouns such as "they" in reference to students at the University of Toronto who didn't identify as either male or female. This regardless of whether Canadian law tried to force him to or not. While at first glance some sensitive soul might mistake this stand for an expression of so-called transphobia, the situation seemed substantially more complex than that.

If the Canadian "Bill C-16"—which would criminalize hate speech against gender expression and gender identity—was passed, it would, in Peterson's view, be the first time in Canada's one-hundred-fifty-year history that someone could be taken to court for *not* using certain expressions; for *not* following the linguistic decrees imposed by those whom Peterson regarded as authoritarian and radical-left so-called social justice warriors. Peterson even believed that, by extension, subjects like biology could become impossible to teach, as it would no longer be *legal* to claim that there were biological differences between men and women without that fact possibly being perceived as a slur—and thereby potentially a form of hate speech or hate crime.

As such, Bill C-16 could represent a serious curtailment

of citizens' fundamental freedom of expression. Peterson was staunch in his conviction. Should he be fined—which was clearly a risk if he refused to use gender-neutral pronouns at his students' behest—then he certainly had no intention of paying them, and should he get sent to prison, then his intention was to go on hunger strike, perhaps not unlike IRA member Bobby Sands at Maze Prison in Northern Ireland in the 1980s. Not that I believe Peterson meant to draw any parallel between himself and Sands (or any other political martyr who died of self-starvation)—at least not publicly—but it didn't seem at all implausible that Peterson genuinely shared Sands's readiness to die for his cause.

Overnight, Peterson had become famous for his opposition to trends in the humanities that had been making the rounds for some thirty years, more or less. Many people in the academic world probably felt it was high time someone took a stand, even if they didn't yet dare say so openly. For Peterson in any case, Bill C-16 had been the match in the powder keg.

In my not-altogether-exhaustive research, I myself had come to ponder certain unmistakably tendentious signs of our times. On closer reflection, they were, in fact, impossible to avoid. One could now identify (or perhaps happen to *be identified*, more like) as "cis gender" in a "cis-normative" hegemony. Heterosexuality and capitalism were tyranny. White people obviously had "white privilege," and those who weren't white were "racialized" as Black or "non-white," and by definition subordinated and oppressed by majority society. This was all a crying shame for those blameless minorities, who couldn't possibly be racists or anti-Semites themselves. Rather, they were, without exception, the victims of a corrupt and intrinsically wicked, patriarchal, oppressive Western civilization—and if they ever made any mistake, it was basically not their fault. A "sans papier" was always holy or downright sacrosanct.

"Intersectionality" was the order of the day. And if you couldn't see that you were *dumb*. According to Swedish Wikipedia, a so-called intersectional analysis was based on postmodern feminist theory, queer theory, postcolonial theory, and Black feminism. The point of intersectional analysis, it said, was not only to shed light on how divergent, subordinated, or marginalized identities (a.k.a. the "racialized," "homosexual," or "working class") were produced in the so-called intersections between such categories; it was also to call attention to how "whiteness," "heterosexuality," and "the upper class" operated as so-called identity categories.

With a concept like intersectionality, academics—not to mention culture journalists, politicians, et cetera—had been given carte blanche to fully devote themselves to their bellyaching, paranoid fantasies about the world. It was all nonsense, clearly. Identity politics hadn't necessarily been nonsense from the start, I thought, but when it eventually got institutionalized and McDonaldized, this theory, too—founded on neo-Marxist obsessions about oppressors and the oppressed in *literally every kind of context*—became patently idiotic, an obvious tool for more or less half-baked opportunists and political activists. I truly couldn't see it any other way.

It was around this time, that is, 2017–18, that curious debates might appear in the tabloid press about trans people's existence or nonexistence. In an article that I'd saved on my phone, one self-styled feminist activist attested that young lesbian feminists were now being accused of transphobia if they didn't want to have sex with lesbian trans women who had penises. Since trans women were women and absolutely nothing else, according to the trans activists, their genitalia should no longer be considered as masculine or feminine attributes—but instead as "girldicks." This was, to my knowledge, the first time that I'd come across this peculiar and yet strangely *stimulating* term. *Girldicks.* In all honesty I found it both provoking and titillating.

If the young lesbian feminists held firm in their sexual preference for biological women, the writer alleged, then the intractable trans activists would simply retort that they were "vagina fetishists," thereby transforming them into so-called *terfs*; that is, *trans-exclusionary radical feminists*. What a time to be alive. Sexual orientation was basically just "a social construct based on stereotypes." All in all, a large-scale—perhaps even global—*mindfuck* was raging unchecked, and since most of these theories and analyses were undoubtedly sanctioned by political correctness and the middle class's blue-eyed value fanaticism, it definitely wasn't something that anyone could oppose—unless, that is, they fancied being a pariah.

A more structural explanation for the increased prevalence of pure idiocy (and downright *deceit*)—at least when it came to Swedish universities—unquestionably came back to funding, and the new governance systems' influence on operations. The 1990s had seen a sea change in the seats of learning, as funding started to be allocated based on student flows. The more students who graduated, the more money each individual institution would receive. Universities, in short, became very keen to meet students halfway. This new system, *New Public Management* (NPM), which sooner or later risked turning the majority of the middle class into the *precariat*, would see students turned into customers. And should this overcosseted education consumer no longer wish to be confronted with reality in any shape or form, then they certainly shouldn't have to be. Ergo so-called *safe spaces*.

Resident Evil: The Final Chapter, which we'd watched the previous night, had, to my great joy, been *exactly as bad and as good* as I'd expected. And, truth be told, it was actually this film more than Peterson or the quandaries of contemporary academia that had been on my mind as I'd sat, on that astoundingly beautiful and tropical morning, drinking my coffee from one of Maria's (fetishistically prized) Moomin mugs.[*] The sun's rays were so strong, its heat so intensely fierce, that it actually felt as though the god Helios had a bone to pick with us mere ephemera, some score to settle.

The *Resident Evil* series of six films had grossed over USD 1 billion, despite the critics not quite being convinced. I could see why they wouldn't care for such unremittingly commercial products. They were way too *lowbrow* for those who considered themselves learned.

After I'd explained to Maria, who was listening with half an ear or perhaps none at all, that it was hardly coincidence that the lead in the film, much like Alice in *Alice in Wonderland*, was named Alice—and, much like Lewis Carroll's young heroine, found her adventures down a rabbit hole (or in Umbrella Corps's "chthonic," i.e., underground, research facility)—she told me with a yawn that the film wasn't at all as scary as I'd originally made it out to be. That much was true. It hadn't actually been all that scary at all—and perhaps, I thought, that might even be one of the reasons why I liked the *Resident Evil* series. The films were too unrealistic—and possibly too bad—to be truly nasty, but that didn't bother me in the slightest, the

---

*Moomin mugs are ceramic mugs featuring illustrations of the Moomin characters, created by Finnish-Swedish author and illustrator Tove Jansson (1914–2001). Moomins are friendly and whimsical creatures resembling white, roundish, hippo-like "trolls" who inhabit the fictional Moomin Valley. The mugs, produced by Arabia Finland, are popular collectibles and could possibly be said to represent markers of a sophisticated and cultured taste among the urban middle class in Scandinavian countries.

reverse if anything, especially given that I wasn't all that into horror films generally. But *Resident Evil* did nonetheless have qualities that appealed to me. One of these qualities—rather, the absolute most crucial of a number of qualities—as far as I was concerned—being: *Milla Jovovich*.

That I had a massive crush on Milla Jovovich was of course not something I was keen to confess to Maria as we lay curled up on the sofa having a nice time in front of the TV. If for no other reason than that I reckoned she'd get jealous, offended, or—well, just moody.

"Jovovich is starting to get on a bit," she'd said at one point, strikingly *caustically*, almost as though she'd guessed I had a soft spot for the lead after all.

"Hmm, maybe her age *is* catching up with her a bit," I'd replied, since Maria was right, I guess, even if I was mildly offended on Jovovich's behalf.

Born in 1975, Jovovich was almost ten years my senior and almost fifteen years older than Maria. Purely objectively, Jovovich was undoubtedly an extremely beautiful person. But there was something about my largely unbalanced feelings toward her that I couldn't quite put my finger on. In any case, for some reason I had the unshakable impression that she was *a generally bang-up person*. I imagined that in private she would be *completely unpretentious* and, I suspected, fairly or possibly *very intelligent*. Perhaps even a smart strategist; a pretentious person would never take part in *Resident Evil*. She had almost certainly been turned on, in a manner of speaking, by the same things that turned me on about the *Resident Evil* concept as a whole. It was a good concept. Obviously. A very good concept. A bit mindless, sure—though I'd probably argue *just mindless enough*—and also very *suggestive*. That's what I thought.

Incidentally, while giving Maria the hard sell as to why we should make *Resident Evil* our Friday-night film, I'd mentioned Jovovich as little as possible. In fact, I'd even made out I couldn't remember her name: "That one . . . Milla . . . oh, you know, Milla whatshername . . . the main girl"—"Milla Jovovich?"— "Yeah, maybe. Jo—? *Huh?*"—"Milla *Jo-vo-vich*," she repeated, impatiently and a tad suspiciously.

Nor was I capable of concealing my infantile fascination for as successful a franchise as *Resident Evil*. Perhaps because success generally had such a strong pull on me.

Anyway, as already mentioned, this was the morning on which Maria would, for the last time, perform her gag involving Molly, or the "Molly Joke" as I liked to call it. It had been pretty charming when she'd done it in previous days, but also a little warped and weird, almost so much so that an outsider would probably find it moronic. But I suspect many couples have any number of shady quirks up their sleeves, of which several could very well bear *folie à deux*–adjacent traits.

It would go like this: Maria would use Molly, her little Pomeranian, as a sort of ventriloquist's doll while bobbing

her up and down on her knee, from which Molly would sur-
vey the table with a both vacant and strangely focused gaze.
Molly spoke with a highly affected yet dim-witted voice that
sounded surprisingly funny in Maria's Stockholm accent. This
had happened a number of mornings in a row, and always at
the breakfast table, where we shared the *Svenska Dagbladet*.
When Molly/Maria commented on certain articles, it created
a madcap form of satire, I'd thought at first, since obviously
Molly didn't care that Donald Trump was slapping tariffs on
steel or aluminum for protectionist reasons, but the entire
premise of the comedy was that everything the US president
did simply *horrified* Molly in a completely unhinged way. And
because Molly also had nerve or possibly even brain damage
that meant that her little body was almost constantly shaking
or vibrating (her genes would not be passed on), it was extra
funny that Maria played her as a querulous nervous wreck. In
her exasperation at everything that the American president
did, Molly reflected the real-life political establishment, which
by that point saw in Trump Hitler's equal, more or less. To top
it all off, Molly/Maria had an extremely filthy mouth. Yes, at
times wholly obscene.

But, as with so many things, even the Molly Joke had a
best-by date, and, for all its charms, on that day it would feel—
at least for me—that that date had passed and then some.

It all started with Molly pointing out a relatively posh ad for
plastic surgery—only, as the ad had a distinct whiff of gentility
to it, there was no mention of the word *surgery*—and, after a

bit of banter about the ad, she started heckling Maria for having such small breasts, as though to say that she should get a boob job.

I was slightly thrown by this, but since it was always so funny when Maria threw her voice in that way (plus she really milked the Stockholm slang, which I always got a kick out of), I thought that laughter was legitimate here, too, especially seeing as it felt reasonable to assume that Maria was aware that she was using Molly as a sort of *vehicle* to poke fun at herself and was therefore—presumably—completely okay with it. And Molly was right: Maria's breasts were indeed not large.

But then it was as though the joke started to get a bit out of hand, especially seeing as Molly didn't move on but instead kept ragging Maria about how flat-chested she was, like a manic loon, and I can't deny it was then that I started to suspect that all that stuff about her diminutive breast size might be some kind of *issue* for Maria.

At which point Molly took things even further, and to my mind way too far, by starting to insinuate that one of the main reasons why "Mumma's boyfriend"—that is, me—was even interested in Maria to begin with was because "the gal," as Molly suddenly called her, was "almost as flat as a bloke, innit."

"I think you're laying it on a bit fucking thick there, Maria," I said with an authoritative and possibly wounded tone.—"Huh, what do you mean?" Maria replied in her normal voice.—"Just because *you've* got an issue with your breasts doesn't mean you have to take it out on me?"—"But I haven't got any issues," Maria lied.

But, it soon emerged, it was possible that she may indeed have *had* one, in the past, that is, she could maybe, *maybe* admit as much, but that was "ages ago now." And besides, Molly was the one who'd said it, not her, she tried.

"Jesus Christ, Maria," I said, then slipped a nicotine pouch under my upper lip before going on: "It's *you* who . . . for fuck's sake, *you're* Molly."—"Yeah, but you've said shitty things as Molly, too," Maria countered.—"I have no recollection of ever being Molly," I replied soberly. But, sure enough, I did soon recall having sat there with Molly on my knee just a few days before, distorting my voice in that very same way. (Incidentally, an almost perfect imitation of Maria, if I do say so myself.)

"Okay, so maybe I have been Molly once or twice," I admitted. "But I didn't say shitty things about *you*, did I? Surely I didn't go so far as *personal attacks*?"—"But come on, that was hardly a personal attack!" Maria said in defense.

"Isn't that exactly what it was?"

We'd gone on like that for a while. Back and forth. A kind of argument, and at the same time maybe not. It was hard to overlook the fact that the entire disagreement could be traced back to a bizarre joke involving a very little dog who was blissfully ignorant of what was actually going on.

So anyway, Maria lifted Molly down onto the floor. The little dog darted off to her pink water bowl and started drinking like there was no tomorrow. After which Maria brought up the fact that on several occasions I had indeed expressed a certain fascination for her, if not entirely masculine, then at least *androgynous* features. Something that I was probably prepared to agree with, to some extent. Although I didn't think of Maria as *androgynous*, exactly, it was undeniable that she had pretty narrow hips and a more boyish than generically womanly little arse; she was also pretty tall (for a woman) and slim, sporty, and, at least for the time being, had short, bleach-blond hair. Besides which she was, as Molly had so defiantly pointed out, more or less—albeit not completely—"flat."

Maria then reminded me, as though in passing, that just a week or so before, after we'd been out with Johannes and Olivia one night, I'd asked her if she was my "little Hitler Youth," which she'd thought was pretty "bonkers."

"'Are you my little Hitler Youth?' Yes, that's what you asked me, and then you . . . uh . . . stroked me." She didn't look at me as she said this but kept her eyes fixed on *Svenskan*, turned the page cool as a cucumber, took a sip of juice.

For a few seconds I didn't have a clue what she was on about. But then, when it hit me that I had indeed asked her if she was my "little Hitler Youth," while stroking her short hair with what I'd felt was an overly stiff or rigidly fascistoid tenderness (like a highly depraved youth leader circa 1933), I surprisingly enough felt a wave of shame flood through me. It was true. On that night she'd been wearing shorts, a crinkled, short-sleeved brown blouse, and old-school braces. It was all exceedingly *vintage*, and we'd gotten back to her apartment, both pretty drunk, and started making love right there in the hall. She'd gotten down on her knees and for some time I'd just stood there pressing her face to my crotch as I stroked the cropped hair at the nape of her neck. I'm not sure if the shame was so much about what I'd said, or what had happened after. That the shame nevertheless reared its ugly head could be due to the fact that, until Maria reminded me of it, I'd simply forgotten the whole thing. Plus there was the fact that Maria—who didn't usually tend to kick up a fuss—was now saying she'd found it "bonkers," which I was struggling slightly to understand. Yes, those were her exact words, that she'd found it "pretty bonkers," which I mean I didn't really get because I remembered—albeit with a certain dreamlike quality—that her eyes had twinkled and she'd given a little chuckle while answering in the affirmative, and that then, with me still caressing her in that robotlike way, she'd pulled down my zipper and started sucking me off. That is, that in that moment she had quite simply been, if momentarily, the one we were (or at least I was) pretending she was.

Then I also regretted that I'd choked her a little, in jest. Not at all that hard, *nota bene*, but I thought that perhaps that was part of the problem, too, if there was indeed a problem here, since clearly the combination of a bit of pretend-choking and asking her if she was my little Hitler Youth—which I suspect I'd also done with a peculiar hardness to my voice—was possibly crossing some sort of line in her eyes. But on the other hand I hadn't felt like she'd been turned off by it all while the "act" had been in progress—the opposite, more like.

In any case, I felt bruised. I also thought it was pretty low of Maria to use Molly to somehow . . . well, I didn't really know what she was after. Which is precisely why I also added that "Molly" had an obviously proletarian taste in women, especially given how fucking obsessed she was with "big tits." It was a sociological fact, I insisted, noted by Alfred Kinsey no less, in his *Sexual Behavior in the Human Male.*

Since Maria wasn't familiar with the Kinsey reports, I had to fill her in. Well aware that at any second I could be whacked with an accusation of *mansplaining*, I told her that people with a higher education, according to Kinsey's reports from the 1950s, that is, weren't as fixated on large breasts as those who lacked a higher education. In other words, there was a pretty big chance that your average scrubber, say, a typical lager lout, would compulsively appreciate big "knockers" to a much greater degree than an "aristocrat." Maria found this pretty funny. But she also complained, perhaps entirely correctly, that at the end of the day she was more of a paid-up member of the bourgeoisie than me.

To which I couldn't help but comment that I found it regrettable that Maria was—consciously or not—using the Molly Joke to let unprocessed episodes from her subconscious rear up from behind a Molly facade. But then she accused me of doing exactly the same thing. She said that Molly even sounded more or less "racist" when in my clutches, as it were.

I then reminded her that she'd laughed so much she'd almost fallen off her chair when Molly had been "a bigot," and that it was objectively funny regardless. In fact, I could tell from the look on her face—as we sat there at the kitchen table arguing about it—that she still thought that joke about unaccompanied minors had been a hoot! Which she, with a shrug, finally conceded that it had. Whatevs.

Then she admitted, in an entirely different tone of voice, that she didn't really have anything against her own appearance, au contraire. Having small breasts was a good thing, more or less, except for when it came to mammograms, but still, she acknowledged, she "might" have liked to have slightly bigger breasts, or perhaps she even went so far as to say "real" breasts—especially when she'd been "young and stupid" as it were. Fact was, she'd been more or less bullied by girls with bigger boobs in secondary school, and that . . . well, perhaps that could have surfaced while she was being Molly.

Which in turn made me acknowledge—since I was starting to feel increasingly sorry for the flat-chested Maria of days gone by—that I, like Molly had said, had to at least some extent been attracted by Maria's "androgynous appearance." But that my feelings for her "on a deeper level" didn't *solely* lie in her in any way looking like a dude, no way. And it was actually, I said, completely "out of line" for her to claim anything of the sort, and not least "a little insulting to me" that she saw things that way. Since if I *was* more interested in being with a guy than a girl—then I'd . . . well, I'd just do it, no?

At the end of the day, neither I nor Maria was completely averse to bisexuality, I thought. So what was even the issue? Why had I felt so *shook*—if I'm using that word *du jour* correctly—at our furry little friend (or, rather, Maria) saying all that stuff about me being turned on by her because she was "almost flat as a bloke"?

Why had I more or less overlooked—or "repressed" I should say for accuracy's sake—that I'd asked her if she was "my little Hitler Youth"?

Just then—as this episode played out at Maria's kitchen table one exceedingly beautiful May morning—these were questions I had pretty much zero intention of making any real effort to answer, but . . . well, they would haunt me for a while. Yes, even the question of why, in the heat of the moment, so to speak, that is, after we'd been out with Johannes and his on-off girlfriend, Olivia, and started getting hot and heavy right there in the hall, I'd associated her specifically with a Hitler Youth or perfect Aryan beauty—yes, that did, I thought, perhaps merit some contemplation—for my own sake, if nothing else. In any case, it was then and there that the gag involving Molly, or what I, as previously mentioned, had liked to call the "Molly Joke"— which had once been so funny, but now no longer was—died.

3

JOHANNES'S NEIGHBOR

As I sat some days later at Plankan, waiting for my friend Johannes, who had promised to lend me the copy of *12 Rules* that he had recently bought (but claimed he hadn't yet had the energy to tackle), an unusually elegant and well-heeled couple suddenly stepped into my local. It was a Sunday afternoon and the weather was—as usual that spring—almost scarily good. There wasn't a cloud in the sky, and the temperature was alarmingly high.

The clearly well-to-do couple were in an exuberant mood, and even seemed a little drunk.

Initially I got the feeling that they were tourists, possibly from Stockholm (or perhaps a much more affluent part of Gothenburg), but their accents were extremely hard to place.

They sat down next to me at the bar, ordered two glasses of cava, and then informed Anna the waitress that it had just come out that Jean-Claude Arnault (a.k.a. the "Cultural Profile" in the Swedish media) once had the temerity to grope even Princess Victoria's bum.[*]

I would say that they appeared to be at once amused and dismayed by this news. As they seemed so open to striking up a conversation, and hadn't gotten the response they'd expected from Anna, who probably wasn't all that interested in the scandals surrounding the Swedish Academy—and who in her defense was stressed and had her hands full with the orders from the jam-packed outdoor seating area—where just the previous weekend at least two guests, she'd informed me, had fainted due to sunstroke—I couldn't help but ask where the couple had gotten that shocking tidbit.

"It was in today's *Svenskan*!" they chimed in chorus.

I wasn't especially surprised. It felt only too plausible given what I had previously heard about this man. His boundlessness, his physically oriented version of Tourette's, was so "democratic" that it clearly wouldn't be limited to the plebs: even princesses were, as had just been demonstrated, fair game for "unwelcome advances."

---

[*]Arnault is a French-Swedish photographer and former artistic director of a cultural center in Stockholm, married to a member of the highly regarded Swedish Academy. The media's scrutiny of his activities attracted a lot of attention during this time, hardly surprisingly leading to a great scandal: Arnault was later found guilty of two sexual assaults and sentenced to two years and six months in prison.

Incidentally, the couple were the only complete strangers I'd met by then who were the least bit interested in the scandal. It therefore seemed quite significant that they were so posh. Presumably, the more that people identified with the Academy and its aristocratic vibes, the more likely they would be to care about the catastrophe that had struck that feudal institution. Me, I couldn't help but immediately express my misgivings that the Nobel Prize in Literature would be impossible to award that year.

"It's quite possible, as someone wrote a while back," I said with a slightly solemn tone, "that it might all be seen as a *bribe* of eight million kronor or whatever the prize money is. As I'm sure you know, people have started to question the Academy internationally, too." They nodded in agreement.

"Though it's worth questioning whether the Academy's position and status weren't already damaged before the 'Cultural Profile' and #MeToo. At least according to writer Pierre Assouline, a member of the jury that awards the Prix Goncourt.

"First they gave the prize to that Russian journalist Svetlana Alexievich, whom I do consider *nobélisable* in a way, but given that she's actually a journalist, it was undeniably a clear departure from their tradition of giving the prize to purely literary writers. Then they gave it to that so-called song-and-dance man Bob Dylan. Because he, as Sara Danius, then-permanent secretary of the Academy put it, is 'good at rhyming.'

"A clear error," I said and went on: "Peter Handke, who by the way is persona non grata in cultural circles because of his defense of Milošević, said that Dylan most likely considered the prize an all-out insult. Assouline thought Danius should have stepped down as permanent secretary right then and there, and I wholeheartedly agree."

The elegant couple, who perhaps hadn't given the matter quite this much thought, once again nodded in agreement. They seemed, I thought, pretty pleased to find someone in this old working-class quarter (Majorna) who was as well versed in these matters as I must claim I was. But at the same time I got the sense that they didn't know who Handke was, and that they perhaps weren't actually all that bothered about the recent winners of the Nobel Prize in Literature.[*]

When Johannes eventually arrived he looked visibly rattled. At the very least I could see in him a certain keenness to get something off his chest. So after I'd taken my leave of the elegant, well-dressed pair and we'd slung ourselves down in the corner with a couple of cold ones—my second, Johannes's first—he started recounting one of the most arresting stories I've ever heard.

For a few years now, Johannes had lived in a studio with a bathroom and kitchenette over on the other side of Majorna. He was happy in the place, even though he quite often complained that it was actually starting to get too small for him. So

---

[*]Incidentally, Peter Handke was awarded the same prize in 2019.

anyway, about six months earlier, he'd suddenly noticed that the door of the closet in his front hall, the frame of which went almost all the way up to the ceiling, was unusually difficult to open and close, and it had visibly started to catch against the ceiling.

He hadn't thought much of it. Subsidence, he reasoned, was par for the course in older buildings in Gothenburg; virtually the entire city was built on clay or marshland. Anyway, time had passed, and besides, he might not even have used that closet in a month or two. It was only when he'd tried to do so earlier that week that he'd discovered it wouldn't open at all.

Upon closer inspection, he'd noticed that the ceiling itself had started to sag or warp slightly in that particular area of the hall, literally barricading the closet door shut. Completely. "Has the ceiling swelled in some way?" he told me he'd wondered. Anyway, the whole thing hadn't felt natural. So after a while he felt compelled to go up to his neighbor to see what was going on, since, given that he couldn't open his closet door at all, and his ceiling was visibly sagging or warping, it was increasingly looking like it was possibly—or definitely, more like—or very likely indeed—a case of water damage. So he went upstairs and rang his neighbor's doorbell.

What Johannes would come to witness when his neighbor finally opened the door was, in his own words, the worst thing he had seen in his life. His neighbor's floor was one great big damp mass, or rather mush, of rubbish, old newspapers and pizza boxes, packaging and food waste and more. And this mass of damp waste was crawling with spiders. Not little ones, mind, but *proper* spiders. Whacking great spiders. And not just a few, or two or three, but *lots* of them. Masses of spiders. I shuddered.

With a nervy courteousness his neighbor had invited him inside, but for a few seconds Johannes had been incapable of doing anything but just stand there, *completely paralyzed*, at the door. Once he'd regained control of his body he'd taken a few steps back into the stairwell, until he could no longer see the devastation within the flat.

Johannes was of the opinion that it clearly must have taken a very long time to produce the level of disorder that he had borne witness to. All the while, a mere few feet below this horror show, he had been going about his daily life, wholly oblivious to his neighbor's complete insanity.

Granted, even before then he'd found his neighbor a little strange or odd, sure, but never in his life would he have suspected him of being as seriously mentally ill as he clearly was.

That something was wrong with the ceiling he had kind of suspected for a while but not given too much thought; as mentioned above, it wasn't unusual for an old building in Gothenburg to have subsidence issues.

The neighbor had followed him out into the stairwell and then launched into a quasi confession about his living situation. Of course, he'd wanted to clean up for ages, absolutely, 100 percent, but in the end it had all gotten to be too much, completely unmanageable, so he'd just turned a blind eye to it all. Then, to top it all off, his toilet had gotten blocked, so he'd been using the sink instead, had somehow managed to press his excrement down the drain. But the overflow from the toilet had spread to the hall and . . . well . . . ruined everything and made it all worse. Utterly.

After this short, shocking visit to his neighbor's door, Johannes had immediately contacted the landlord, who had naturally reacted with grave alarm. The very next day Johannes had heard details from the landlord about the flat in which my friend hadn't set foot, but of which he had nevertheless seen quite enough to get a certain idea of its monstrous state. Over time, the landlord had said, the layer of increasingly soggy rubbish on the floor had come to be maybe ten or twelve inches thick.

The neighbor, unsurprisingly, was evicted with immediate effect. The landlord promptly reported the issue to social services, as the man was clearly in need of some sort of help and support. Johannes felt sorry for him. Fact was, he said, his neighbor was often clean and put together, even well dressed, and generally came across as a fully normal Swedish man in his early thirties. It shocked him that this person had been living in such horrific conditions for months but had nevertheless managed to maintain a rudimentary form of hygiene.

Anyway, for Johannes it hadn't ended there. The day after the visit, when the landlord had come to kick out his neighbor and change the locks, his neighbor had rung Johannes's doorbell—the doorbell of the man who had "exposed" this, his bottomless misery, no less—and, in a state of agitation, had asked him to temporarily hold the porn DVDs that he'd collected over the years. While Johannes had refused to let the—by the looks of things—several-kilos-heavy carrier bag over his threshold (understandably enough, he wanted no physical contact with anything belonging to that man), he had eventually agreed to stash the bag in his basement storage space for a few days, max.

So he and his neighbor—or, indeed, *ex*-neighbor—whose most-prized possession was clearly this porn stash, had together taken the long walk down to the basement storage room.

Johannes made no bones of the fact that he'd been fearful of this strange person (even if, purely physically, he thought he had the upper hand)—but thankfully nothing had happened, and on the day we met the neighbor had returned, picked up the goods, and thanked him dearly for the favor. The whole thing had ended without drama, and their paths would probably never cross again.

He went on to tell me that the landlord had already towed a huge skip into the courtyard and started the decontamination. Johannes had seen a whole troop of men in substantial overalls and gloves begin tossing everything out: the furniture, sink, toilet, kitchen cabinets, fridge, and freezer; in short, the whole shebang. Since the flat was relatively small it hadn't taken all that long. According to the landlord, Johannes's ceiling would probably need replacing sooner or later, and if so he would

have to move out for a while. They offered to find him temporary accommodation in a nearby hotel (presumably the three-
star Spar Hotel in Majorna), unless he by any chance might be
able to stay with friends or family.

"Fact is, Johannes," I conceded, "I don't think I've ever heard
a story as creepy and disgusting as that." It was true. Several
aspects—details—of the story had immediately etched themselves into my mind, and—I assumed—for life: the layer of
rubbish on the floor that had formed a thick, wet sludge; the
spiders; his neighbor's collection of deeply treasured pornog-
raphy.

Johannes agreed: "Yeah, it *was* fucking nasty, I can tell you
that. Just the fact that I lived under it so long without the slightest idea what was going on upstairs . . . Yeah, I guess it says
something about humanity's extreme isolation in big cities. It's
fucking unhealthy!"

Incidentally, on several occasions over that summer I would
ask Johannes to retell the entire "Story of the Neighbor," as I
instantly came to call it. Indeed, I practically coaxed him into
doing it. It was as if the "Story" never got old; it continued to
shock and fascinate me. For a while I got the shivers just thinking about it.

When we sat there in the corner at Plankan that day, my
shivers were mostly pure disgust, sure, but I would still say they
weren't exclusively unpleasant. I think they were almost like . . .
well, like the feeling you get from reading Stephen King. The

hairs stand up on the back of your neck—but that's also what you *want* to happen. At the same time, it was perhaps true that this story had a . . . well, largely *existential* quality.

Several things fascinated me about the story. First and foremost, there was probably an involuntary sense of identification there—albeit not so much with Johannes as with his neighbor.

After all, I could quite easily recall that I myself had teetered on the brink of some fairly heavy-duty "scuzziness" in my youth. My flat definitely hadn't been pristine, and I hadn't had any sense of homeliness or feel for home decor; after getting my own place at twenty, for years I'd used a sheet as a curtain and a moving box as a bedside table. Still, the place had obviously never been anything like Johannes's neighbor's place, absolutely not. And yet I saw the image of his neighbor's flat as a metaphor or perhaps archetypal manifestation of a spiritual landscape or state of mind in complete chaos.

"Perhaps your neighbor could have done with this?" I said with a chuckle as I held up Peterson's *12 Rules*. Johannes wasn't particularly amused by the joke I'd allowed myself the liberty of making.

"I doubt it would have helped him."

Truth be told, I suppose the "Story of the Neighbor" stirred a sort of fear within me. It was a dreadful story—and it categorically wasn't fiction or *cock and bull*. The "Story of the Neighbor" illustrated the extent of what humanity was capable of doing to itself, of subjecting itself to. At the same time I felt a palpable sense of gratitude in noting that I, in all likelihood, would never be so mentally ill as to be capable of destroying my own room—my very self—in the same near-monstrously *fanatical* way in which Johannes's neighbor had destroyed his room and himself.

But then again: How could I be so sure?

A regular by the name of Sixten, a lawyer, came in for a beer and sat down with us. This put paid to the "Story of the Neighbor" for that night. Sixten lived just a stone's throw from Plankan and was periodically a pretty frequent patron. He was more an acquaintance of Johannes's than mine, really, but I'd met him a few times myself and liked him a lot, perhaps because I was impressed that he was a lawyer. That Sixten had, for some obscure reason, a particular fondness for Johannes was clear. Granted, Johannes did have a slightly folksier style, one might say; he was more *likable*.

Sixten told us that things had been pretty chill at work and he was grateful for that, as his teenage daughter was, for reasons he didn't go into, currently in need of a lot of support. He explained that it was usually only toward the end of summer that his clients tended to file for divorce, as that was normally when they couldn't put up with each other anymore. Summer holidays, with all their boozing and stress, tended to be the drop that made the cup runneth over. Similarly, after Christmas and New Year's he tended to get a lot of work. A *lot*.

Sixten spotted the copy of *12 Rules* that was lying on the

table and immediately owned up to having read it. He liked Jordan B. Peterson.

"But he's no great thinker," he said.

We were all in agreement there. Still, that notwithstanding, he was, we argued, probably the only contemporary thinker that even so-called normal folk talked about. Even people at Plankan. Sixten had also listened to the episode of *The Joe Rogan Experience* (that I'd listened to on Johannes's advice) and agreed that it was in these face-to-face conversations that Peterson really came into his own.

Johannes felt that Peterson's greatest intellectual contribution thus far had been to describe how men select men based on their own hierarchies, and women based on theirs (which weren't entirely independent of the men's [and vice versa?]).

"Men don't turn to women for advice on who should be their leaders."

In a way it felt like stating the obvious, I thought. It was undoubtable that male *and* female hierarchies existed. Sometimes they would overlap; sometimes they wouldn't. In any case, we could agree that Peterson served as a sort of instructional figure, and if his lectures meant that more people started reading some of the great thinkers he made reference to—Friedrich Nietzsche, Carl Jung, Mircea Eliade, Joseph Campbell, and so on—then that would nevertheless be an important contribution to popular education. Old Media perpetually viewed him as a more-or-less radioactive character, but sooner or later they would have to take the phenomenon that he had become seriously. Their pathetic attempts to paint him as an alt-right figure, a Nazi or fascist, wouldn't pan out in the long run. Anyone who actually listened to him could tell that those were horrendous exaggerations, which, we believed, would gradually undermine trust in any media that persisted in pretending that the world hadn't changed a jot since YouTube.

"They'll never regain the power they once had," Johannes said. "Those days are gone."

Sixten then got onto how marriage had long been a dying institution, and that "coupledom" was increasingly starting to become one, too.

"Young people aren't getting married anymore. In any case not in any great numbers. They move in together, have kids, stick together a few years—best case ten, let's say—then split up. A clear trend. Perhaps primarily among the lower classes."

While I demurely questioned if that was such a "bad deal," really, Johannes emphatically insisted that it absolutely was a bad deal, a really fucking bad deal—at least for the kids who would likely pay a high price for the absence of a father in their lives.

It turned into a pretty short session. Sixten downed his beer and left, and Johannes handed over Peterson's book with a warning that he would kill me if I lost it, which I certainly had no intention of doing. Then he set off for Olivia's place in Lunden, where he was going to spend a few days—he couldn't take being in his own flat right now. As for me, I ordered another beer, flicked absent-mindedly through *12 Rules*, and continued digesting the story that Johannes had told me. But after half the beer I went back to my place, seriously pondering why the "Story of the Neighbor" had elicited such a strong reaction within me.

It wasn't just that I personally (retroactively) identified with young men who were a little lazy and had untidy rooms, or at the very least were sorely lacking in any flair for home decor; for several years now I had also—I recalled—had recurring nightmares about rooms, studios, apartments, and buildings that to some degree matched the veritable shop of horrors that Johannes had conjured up before my eyes with regard to his neighbor's unspeakable flat.

These were nightmares that I had had so often, and been so fixated on, that I'd even developed a kind of dedicated vocabulary to describe them. They revolved around what I termed *debased*, *destroyed*, and *demolished* rooms; spaces that in a *spiraling*—or *derailed*—way would, over the course of the dream, become all the more amoral and degenerate. Occasionally I myself would inhabit these rooms, studios, or entire apartments, which were without exception extremely scuzzy, exceedingly derelict, and not infrequently teeming with insects, worms, rats, and not least *spiders*.

It always felt as though some evil and unnamable internal or external force—perhaps a *daimon*—wanted to inflict upon these dwellings—or rather me, my person—substantial harm.

Indeed, in a way I'd already come to the conclusion that the only truly sound (psychoanalytical) interpretation of these dreams of *debased*, *destroyed*, and *demolished* rooms was that they were in fact a sort of manifestation of a potential moral ruin within me. A sort of Residence of Shadows. That they were my subconscious's manifestations of what I really was, or—worst-case scenario—had the potential to become. I suppose that was what made these dreams so angst ridden and, I guessed, in a way as loaded with shame as they were.

Occasionally I would try to clean the spaces in these dreams, but it was hopeless, futile; everything was putrefying, on the brink of collapse, sodden and falling apart, spent and fragmented beyond redemption. The spaces of my nightmares were anything but fit for human habitation. Inside them I was completely alone, paralyzed, helpless. In reality I had never experienced such a space—unless I was repressing the experience, that is—but clearly, it struck me—*clearly* I'd been unhappy in the, at times, perhaps genuinely unclean flat of my younger, hungover, postpubescent days. But in the end I'd managed to get out of that.

As it happened, I hadn't yet made a habit of making my bed, reasoning that it would have felt extremely autistic to do so, but by that summer I was keeping my flat in good enough shape that it didn't immediately signal mental illness; I had, however, invested in proper furniture and household utensils, among other things, and in so doing I suppose I'd also taken control of—or ultimately confronted, I thought—some of the inner demons that I'd had. My self-acceptance was at least sizable enough that I could consider myself deserving of a *decent living environment*. With time I'd also applied to, and been offered, my job as an administrative assistant—a perfectly okay middle-class job— and embarked upon a serious and *sensible* relationship with the fairer sex (in the shape of Maria). I had thereby challenged my fear of intimacy and broken free of my emotional isolation. In short, in recent years I had made some good progress toward becoming a more-or-less "normal" person, so to say.

A *normie*.

It was curious, I kept thinking, a near-mystical coincidence, that Johannes had told his story so soon after I'd binge-read Sigrid Rausing's *Mayhem: A Memoir*,[*] in which the Tetra Pak billionaire wrote exhaustively about her brother Hans Kristian's and his wife Eva Rausing's substance abuse. The couple had met at a rehab center in the USA in the 1980s. Eva was the daughter of a Pepsi group big shot and, like Hans Kristian, had never had to worry about money. They had four children together. Everything had gone well until New Year's Eve 1999, when—knowingly or unknowingly—they had made the mistake of drinking a few glasses of champagne that weren't alcohol-free, after which everything had gone downhill, or rather been shot to absolute shit, for years.

On Monday, July 9, 2012, British police had arrested Hans

---

*In English; the book came out in Swedish translation only later that year (2018), published by Albert Bonniers Förlag.

Kristian on suspicion of possession of so-called class-A drugs, after he'd been caught driving erratically through South London. They had subsequently conducted a search of the forty-nine-year-old philanthropist's £70 million property in Cadogan Place, Belgravia. In a sealed bedroom they had found his wife's body in a bed, hidden beneath a pile of clothes, blankets and duvets, a number of TV screens, some drawers, and a blue tarpaulin. To contain the smell, the billionaire had put duct tape over the cracks around the door. When the story came out it made huge headlines. It would emerge that his wife had lain dead there for over a month.

Despite being written by one of the UK's richest women, I'd found *Mayhem* surprisingly readable and revealing. I would even call it moving, though that sounds like empty praise.

Indeed, it *was* moving. Absolutely. At the same time, I couldn't get away from the fact that the lack of compassion I'd felt for the writer and her family probably stemmed from simple jealousy and perhaps resentment that my own financial situation had become all the more insecure. At a staff meeting at the County Administrative Board just a few weeks earlier, I'd found out that they might be forced to make redundancies, and, as the last one in, I would also by necessity be the first one out. It's true, though, I wasn't the only one affected. Up to a dozen or so administrators and low-level civil servants risked losing their jobs. I saw uncertain times ahead. Shit times.

Once the recession kicked in it would probably be fucking hard to find a *decent* new job. Especially since I had no real qualifications to speak of. For a long time I'd dreamt of earning a living from writing but had never had any real talent for it. Perhaps because I was too eccentric to fit in in the more conventionally literary and arts-journo scenes, where for some time now out-and-out *virtue signaling* had seemed way more important than more classical cultural capital. Nor was money per se anything that motivated me to any great degree. At the same time, the question was whether I'd ever given myself an honest shot at writing; surely it was far easier to live one's life as a low-level staffer than make a serious go of becoming a professional wordsmith?

Compared to Sigrid Rausing, anthropologist, philanthropist, writer, and publisher (owner of *Granta* magazine and Granta Books), most people, even multimillionaires, were basically destitute anyway. She and her family lived in a mansion in central London that had cost £20 million way back in the nineties. The accompanying two-acre garden (i.e., around 87,000 square feet) was the biggest in London that belonged to a private individual. Only the British royal family had a bigger one.

In her memoir, Rausing had used the Freudian concept of *unheimlich*, which is generally used to denote a sinister, uncanny feeling, to describe the paradox of how, in her brother's private palace—all marble finishes and oil paintings lining the walls, in one of the city's most fashionable areas—two worlds had existed side by side: the—as I understood it—(for her own class) completely *homely* and *home-y* luxury; and—concealed—like an extremely obscene toy inside a treacherously innocent chocolate easter egg, or perhaps an egg-shaped piñata, or rather, Fabergé egg—*within* this unparalleled manifestation of status, wealth, prestige, culture, and impeccable taste—its complete, hidden, and *un-home-y* opposite: the rags and tatters of addiction; a veritable cancerous growth.

The first floor had been in immaculate condition, magnificent in every respect, beautiful and decorous, but the bedroom on the second floor was—as Rausing put it—a "squat." Her brother's housekeepers and other staff weren't allowed inside; they would carefully place meals down on a tray outside the door. Then scurry away. In the bedroom, Hans Kristian and Eva had scrawled their dealers' phone numbers straight onto the walls. Food remains, packaging, clothes, and rubbish lay strewn across the floor and a bit all over the place. It was in this *debased*, *destroyed*, and *demolished* room that had once been objectively beautiful, in this almost *spiraling* or *derailed* and increasingly *degenerate* room, that Rausing's sister-in-law had lain dead for week upon week following what doctors presumed was a cocaine overdose. As Eva had had a pacemaker, they could conclude that she had most likely passed at around 7:19 on May 7, when the pacemaker last registered a chaotic heartbeat; a total of nine episodes had been recorded that day, of between 180 and 384 beats per minute.

Obviously I couldn't envy Hans and Eva Rausing's lives in addiction. Their enormous wealth had hardly been of any great help to them. Granted, they were never lacking in money for drugs. But that wasn't only to their advantage. Even Sigrid

Rausing, too, had been caught in the clutches of codependency. Among other things, she describes a pattern of self-harm that saw her cut her own arm in front of her cat, who excitedly caught whiff of the blood, and how after that she had spent time at a rehab center. She had actually been relatively young when this happened.

So I was, naturally, disgusted by my own initial lack of compassion. There was no denying the fact that—despite being rich as trolls—these were people to be pitied, just as Johannes's neighbor was to be pitied, and anyone else who was generally forced to live in real-world environments that corresponded to those I had nightmares about. At the same time, I couldn't help but feel that the Rausings' abject wealth—both Hans Kristian and Sigrid were good for many, many billion—nevertheless challenged or prompted a decrease in the amplitude of my compassion (or even of my feeling for humanity at large). At least if I was being completely honest with myself. These were people of flesh and blood, like me; they were wounded by the same weapons, struck down by the same diseases, cured by the same medicines, and yet . . . something about their wealth, I guess, transformed them into extraterrestrials in my eyes—and it also wasn't completely unreasonable to assume that they, too, might conceivably view themselves as not quite of this world. Especially given the enormous remove at which they lived from the more normative layers of society. Indeed, I thought, there was definitely something *unheimlich*—something genuinely uncanny—about not only what Sigrid Rausing had written about her brother and her sister-in-law's death in their "squat" in the middle of a palace; *there was also something uncanny about such enormous wealth in itself*, and the *mystical* or almost *occult* fantasies it had stirred within me after devouring that extraordinary book.

There was something in that. It resembled the "shift" I'd felt within me when Johannes had recounted the "Story of the Neighbor." As though I'd suddenly found myself in a world of Lovecraftian horror. Indeed, was it not completely possible, I thought as I lay on my leather sofa, flicking through my copy of *Mayhem*, that the enormously wealthy were also affected by these very same uncanny impressions around enormous wealth? And could that not, I reasoned further, have played a role in Eva Rausing's paranoid delusion that her own father-in-law, Hans Rausing, was responsible for the assassination of Swedish prime minister Olof Palme on the streets of Stockholm in 1986?

The possibility, or, rather, risk of—via mental illness and addiction—creating an isolated but more or less well-organized space of total *dissociation* and paranoia *in the midst*, as it were, of this glamourous and commanding institution—or manifestation—of extreme wealth, would reasonably be something that certain inordinately wealthy people would be forced to recognize, be that consciously or subconsciously (and perhaps especially so in a Christian culture in which Jesus's words about it being easier for a camel to pass through the eye of a needle than for a rich man to enter the kingdom of God still remained the original and definitive judgment against richness per se).

This seemed all the more reasonable the more I thought about it. But as it was unlikely that I would ever hobnob with such extremely rich and unusual people—and equally unlikely that I myself would ever be so rolling in it that I would be mentally transformed by such wealth—I supposed that when all was said and done I would never get any *real* insight into their psychology. Even if Sigrid Rausing had kind of given us a peek through the keyhole in her book.

Still, examples of the self-destructive, psychologically scarred, and withdrawn yet fabulously wealthy man (and, more rarely, woman) abounded in both reality and fiction. Film legend Howard Hughes was one such example (and perhaps the best, seeing as he spent the last twenty-five years of his life as a hermit). Michael Jackson was another. One could possibly also mention Bruce Wayne a.k.a. Batman here, at least in Frank Miller's interpretation. Charles Foster Kane in Orson Welles's *Citizen Kane*. Oil magnate Daniel Plainview in Paul Thomas Anderson's *There Will Be Blood*. Insane recluses. Rich, genuinely lost, downright totaled souls. The enormously wealthy, by this hypothesis, were *incapable* of experiencing the world in a way that a so-called *normal person* experiences it.

Money fundamentally changed the enormously wealthy person's *phenomenological* world, their entire *Umwelt*. In a way, Rausing's book did contest this. Not because she seemed exactly average or normal, perhaps, but because she was so capable of formulating her feelings and thoughts in a way that didn't appear particularly *dissociative* or *derealized*, disconnected from or wholly extraneous to my own middle-class experience. And perhaps that went some way to explaining the conflicting emotions I'd felt both while and after reading the book? Sigrid Rausing had challenged my *bias* against the enormously wealthy. Fact was, I hadn't had the slightest intention of seriously exploring (or challenging my prejudices against) these people's *inner worlds* before I'd read her book.

Despite being good for billions—and in my eyes almost resembling another variant of human being (as though *mutated*, in my own [probably] *compensatory* fantasies about the psyches of the rich and powerful)—she and I, I thought, that's to say me and Sigrid Rausing, anthropologist, philanthropist, writer, and publisher, would probably nevertheless be able to sit down somewhere (preferably London) over a cup of tea and have a pleasant and cultivated conversation.

After all, we were largely interested in the same sorts of things: literature, art, and . . . well, maybe *culture* generally. Culture, which, according to Carl Jung, was perhaps the very meaning and purpose of the second half of life (which I had by now inevitably started to approach). Of course Sigrid Rausing was no idiot! Obviously she cared about these things. Even she ought to maximally understand the importance of symbolic and cultural capital and was surely, like myself, (more or less) concerned that the value of book learning, for example, might be cheapened in a world of audiobooks and diminishing literary reading habits among kids, young people, and adults alike. Incidentally, was that not precisely how the papers had once described her—as "the billionaire with 'cultural capital'?"

4

THE MARIA DREAM

As I lounged, some days later, in Maria's Bruno Mathsson armchair, letting my thoughts wander as they pleased, it struck me that I'd probably behaved like a bit of a slut in my highly peculiar dream of the night before. My friend Sigrid Rausing, that's to say anthropologist, philanthropist, and publisher Sigrid Rausing, had leaned in over the table at which we were drinking our Earl Greys and said: "Sanitary towels are *extremely* good, yes, perhaps even complete essentials for any survival kit." So true. Sanitary towels were definitely good to have. I clearly remembered telling her that she was dead, *dead* right there. "Dead, *dead* right!" I'd said, I remembered, and my voice had even quavered slightly, as though I'd been immensely touched by the veracity of her words. Terribly touched. The fawning hadn't stopped there.

"You really are *on it*, Sigrid. You're on it!"—"Yes, I guess I *am* pretty on it with that stuff," the billionaire had replied.—"You definitely are. More on it than anyone I know. Yes, I might as well say it like it is: you *inspire* me! There, I've said it." That might not literally have been how the words had come out in my dream, but it was something along those lines. In any case, I'd been extremely devout in my admiration of the billionaire's expertise on what a decent so-called survival kit— recommended to all citizens by the state-initiated "72 hours" campaign[*]—should contain (though, really, it went without saying that there should be menstrual products in there, especially if you—like Rausing—were a woman, besides the usuals, I mean: water, canned goods, a can opener, a battery-powered radio, solar panels or a generator, a flashlight, candles, matches, etc.), and it was clear that I was shamelessly fishing for a "grant" or some form of kickback. *Surely she'll give me a grant if I'm just nice enough?* I'd thought.

But, as it happens, that particular passage of the dream, or rather *dreams*—in themselves a mishmash of disparate sequences—wasn't what troubled me, even if the shame of my demeaning servility had somehow stuck with me after I'd

---

[*]Seventy-two hours (three days) was the amount of time for which, in the event of a serious national crisis, the Swedish Civil Contingencies Agency (MSB) considered Swedish citizens personally responsible for covering their own basic needs.

woken up at five a.m. feeling completely rested, even though I can't have had more than a few hours' sleep.

After the episode with Rausing, Maria—or at least a kind of version of Maria—and I had stood pissing in cross-streams in the urinals of a grubby pizzeria in some concrete suburb some-where. I hadn't been able to resist sneaking a peek, and when I'd seen how generously endowed she was, I couldn't help but feel a little jealous—and perhaps even fascinated.

Maria could somehow tell that I was in a bit of a funk, feeling on edge in this dicey part of town, so she'd calmed me down by saying she knew loads of "peeps" in "da hood." I could chill, she assured me while nonchalantly holding her semierect member. The place was *soft*, she said. Most of the people there were her "bros or homies," if I "dug" her meaning.

In the dream, Maria had transmuted into what people in early-nineties Sweden would call a "kicker" and was dressed in the appropriate garb for this subculture: a shiny black Adidas tracksuit with emblematic white or possibly yellow stripes down the sides of the sleeves and legs. A white vest and black cap. (Though, yes, in truth it was like dreams usu-ally are: everything fluttering around and shape-shifting, changing color and form, nothing permanent or set in stone; even her cock had actually changed shape and size—at first it was fascinatingly big, as mentioned, only to become off-puttingly small a second later, almost like a large clitoris or a child's penis, before eventually reassuming the shape of a much truer-to-life, sizable phallus. The only thing that stayed the same and unchanged was in fact Maria's bilaterally symmetrical face.)

"I've always been a kicker," said Dream Maria. "It's an *important* part of my identity, you get?" I didn't dare say anything but that I got. "Yeah, I get you, I get you," I mumbled edgily.

Dream Maria commanded respect, and I may even have been a little afraid of her. This was her domain, her *hood*. That much I knew. I wouldn't make it out of there without her. Without her as my guide and interpreter, this "hood" would eat me up. Everyone else could see I was a tourist, a dumb middle-class day-tripper in the *ghetto*.

Dream Maria had then lurched, as though a little drunk (or else just pretending to be), and her face had ended up right next to mine, and I'd gotten even more scared when I caught the whiff of cigs on her breath and also got the unmistakable feeling that she could either headbutt me at any second—since, despite still being pretty slim in the dream, her pointed style of dress radiated a not-insignificant violence capital—*or else* just as easily kiss me.

I once again turned my attention to her cock, noting as I did that her pubic hair was trimmed and she had a massive tattoo across her lower belly of a couple of words in some gothic font, like the *Frankfurter Allgemeine*'s logo, but I couldn't make out what they said due to the LSD-trip floatiness of the letters. I got the sudden impulse to touch her, *and maybe*, I thought in the dream, *just maybe I could do it under the pretext of a stupid joke or something*, but I couldn't quite work up the guts to do it, and then suddenly I realized that *that very thought* was what was written across her belly in that gothic font; that is, considerably more than just a couple of words. I didn't dare touch her. Our relationship was different here. Dream Maria—my grim mentor and helper—was, I reflected, a different person entirely than Reality Maria, so to speak, and if I crossed that line she could probably kill me. Besides, perhaps my desire to touch her was less a need for erotic validation (or even depraved curiosity) and more a longing for acceptance, a desire to be one of Dream Maria's *homies* or a fully-fledged member of Dream Maria's *crew*? (This, however, I only realized later, in the middle of the day; the thought could simply have been an attempt to sublimate everything, a form of neurotic, angsty, retrospective clarification.)

When I recalled these dreams, I cringed slightly; they were undeniably embarrassing. But was it really so strange that I'd dreamt them? After all, the story Johannes had told me about his neighbor (just a few days prior) had made me pull Rausing's *Mayhem* back off the bookshelf.

And all that stuff about survival and home preparedness was all part of my work and everyday life. Though I hadn't been directly involved in the "72 hours" campaign that Rausing and I had discussed in the dream, I was still highly well versed in the complexities of getting the public at large to take their civic responsibility seriously when it came to crisis management. Given that consumer society had functioned for generations without the slightest inkling of any serious disruption, it was hard to make people realize how precarious the system really was. This was a frequently recurring topic of conversation at the Unit. Or "a hard mass-psychology nut to crack!" as my boss, Claes, tended to put it. (I really rated Claes by the way, I've got to say, *en passant*. He was a political scientist, presumably Soc Dem, and hugely well read to boot.) If anything happened internationally that ground food deliveries to a halt, people would start to starve within weeks; our infrastructures, shaped around the principles of just-in-time logistics, no longer allowed for any greater stockpiling of foodstuffs. Shops would sell out of food and water in a matter of hours, especially if panic buying kicked in. Claes often mentioned, perhaps in Rogerian terms, the difficulty of getting the public to "own" these issues. But it's a tough balancing act, he argued; inform people too much—give them too many hard truths—and "the fuckers'll just roll down their blinds." A headache for Claes. Well, for all of us, really. Especially given that seventy-two hours was such an optimistic time frame that most people more in the know considered it more or less pure disinformation. But sure, it was better than nothing. Absolutely.

Nor was it all that strange that I'd dreamt what I had about Maria. She herself (through the medium of Molly) had insinuated that I'd fallen in love with her because of her androgynous traits. Something that may have had a certain grain of truth to it, even if I still wasn't completely convinced. Did Maria automatically look like a boy just because she had small breasts? I think not! Basically, it had been a pretty lousy exaggeration on her part. One other reason why I'd dreamt about a Maria with a cock, or, as I thought, a *phallic* Maria as it were, could possibly be the *piquant* incident that had taken place while we were having sex the night before.

All of a sudden Maria had slipped a finger inside me. It wasn't painful in any way, but it had taken me by surprise, and I'd frozen on the spot (or midthrust or whatever). The very instant I'd registered the penetration (of what I suspect was her ring or perhaps middle finger), my gaze had locked on to her fluffy Totoro toy from the classic Miyazaki anime, who usually kept guard on the bed, and I'd seen that, from his temporary position on the chair in the bedroom, he was staring at me wide-eyed. In his right paw, as usual, he held his little sackcloth bundle, about which I would occasionally speculate as to what it was supposed to contain, and, since Totoro was a kind of forest spirit, a sort of magical creature—like the house elf of Nordic folklore—it might just be possible, I'd conjectured, that the bundle itself was *magical* and could therefore hold basically anything inside: a Shinto temple, a monster truck, or why not even a whole kolkhoz?*

But what had irritated me the most—at least in that moment—was that I hadn't positioned Totoro with his face turned away, since—the very second I felt that finger—it was almost as though . . . indeed, it was almost as though he

---

*A form of collective farm in the Soviet Union.

actually had the nerve to give me a little smirk, a surreptitious smile, or *even laugh*.

In any case, I hadn't exactly blocked Maria's penetration. In a situation such as that, an overly strong or negative reaction would have struck an inconsistent (or downright hypocritical) note, especially given that Maria's own bumhole wasn't exactly a taboo area for her, sexually. For which I was obviously grateful. Still, after a while I'd moved her hand away, for although her finger was slippery and moist with sweat and probably her own lubrication, too, it wasn't all that comfortable and did nothing for me, at least not enough for it to be worth it. In fact, I thought as I thought back on it all, it had been a pretty discreet evasive maneuver on my part; I'd simply changed position to make it too unwieldy for her to reach me; having been inside her, classic missionary, I'd simply taken hold of the backs of her knees and pressed them up as far as they would go, so they were practically up by her ears (something that was likely interpreted as clumsy overegging on my part), all while completely ignoring Maria's raised eyebrows and look of surprise by leaning forward to cover her lips with my own.

When I'd woken up from the dream(s), Maria had been lying beside me, looking the way she normally did when she was in a deep and dreamless sleep. I'd gone into the kitchen and heated up a cup of tea in a Moomin mug with Moomintroll's cheeky lady friend, Snorkmaiden, on it. It was already pretty light out, and I suspected it would be another one of those bizarrely hot days. The weather forecast bore out my suspicions. The temperature was estimated to reach as much as 35 degrees (95 degrees Fahrenheit) by lunchtime. I drank my tea and flicked a little listlessly through *Svenskan*, which had just dropped with a thud onto the hallway floor, but found myself unable to get the dream off my mind. Did I de facto have a fetish for "kickers," for boys from the hood? For kickers who were *shemales*? It was so bizarre I found myself chuckling. Still, I did want to ponder these questions seriously for a second. Was it possible that boys from the hood—in my (as I saw it) genuinely middle-class consciousness—were "the others" in some way? In a way the thought felt way too postmodern, but wasn't there something to it? Weren't the lower classes, I thought, more in tune with their so-called natures, with their bodies and libidos? Were they not in fact *more nature*? More *natural nature* and—well, instinct? Yes, I did in all seriousness think these thoughts, in a moment of complete *uninhibitedness*, before it hit me how bad it would sound if I were ever to air these controversial prejudices to anyone but myself. I then remembered that a Danish woman I'd dated for a while had told me that coarse and simple—and perhaps largely uneducated—men were the best fucks. The best "fuckmachines," so to say. Intellectual men (a category in which she'd clearly lumped my person) were, by contrast, *intellectual men* and were therefore far too thoroughly socialized, too kind and inhibited—indeed, all too self-conscious—to be truly fuckable. Painful though it was, this had made a lot of sense to me. The Dane didn't want a long-term relationship with these simple people. Obviously not. *They're good for fucking, but not so much else!* Even though this was probably true, I'd still gotten the impression she said it mainly by way of consolation. Indeed, perhaps we should simply be less cerebral, I'd thought at the time.

Much less brainy.

Incidentally, Dream Maria had had the same sociolect as someone from a socially deprived area like Bergsjön or thereabouts (i.e., not her usual silver-spoon Stockholm accent). Perhaps she, Dream Maria, had just barely managed to read Zlatan's memoir *I Am Zlatan Ibrahimovic* (ghostwritten by David Lagercrantz) as an unusually demanding part of her otherwise vocational education (cars, haulage, mechanics?), and perhaps she'd even enjoyed it (if she admired Zlatan, that is, which seemed plausible enough given her background), but it didn't seem all that likely that her reading would go much further; it was highly doubtful that she would be borrowing *The Gulag Archipelago*, for instance, or *In Search of Lost Time* from her local library anytime soon.

But why all this fucking prejudice? My misconceptions about this simple working-class-slash-ghetto tomboy (who in Dream Maria's case was also a sort of *shemale*) were, I realized as I drank my tea from the Snorkmaiden mug in those early-morning hours, essentially *class racist*—and that was not good. Which was definitely why I was feeling a little ashamed. Still, when I came to recap these thoughts later on in the day, when feeling comparatively well rested, I would realize that there was an element of truth to them, at least in the sense that they said something about my own almost pathological inferiority complex; the Dane hadn't exactly made any bones of the fact that I was a useless and overly self-conscious fuck. Then again, hadn't there been something deeply *castrative* about my own middle-class upbringing? Hadn't there been an out-and-out *bias* against masculinity in my childhood home? In my father's eyes, to be fixated on violence in the way that some of my classmates were—that is, more explicitly and unreservedly so than me (who was violence-fixated all the same)—would have been bad. Bodybuilders were vulgar and simple, generally speaking. Real meatheads. Schwarzenegger was vain—and, by implication, femme in his vanity. Toy guns were for the kids of the uneducated. Weapon fetishism was pure perversion. Team sports were hooey. I suppose that, for my father, a man should ideally be classically educated, articulate, and humorous, kind of like John Cleese. In fact, my father had all but radiated an irrefutable *no* to an overly strong, stereotypically manifested masculinity. Though I suppose he meant well. And anyway, being an educated, well-adjusted, and "socially competent" middle-class man—which I generally considered myself to be, even if I did lack a fancy PPE degree—was a clear advantage in society. But had I not had to pay all too high a price for this indoctrination? For this all-too-far-reaching *no* to the clichés and excesses of masculinity? Compared to the Dane's fuckable seadogs I felt basically impotent, like a Snorkmaiden with insufficient penis.

As the writer and poet Stig Larsson once observed: "Being a grown man means removing yourself from the role of the nice, well-behaved kid. Because the nice, well-behaved kid can't get a hard-on."[*] He might well have been spot-on there. The kid who refused to throw his eraser at the teacher in middle school was probably the same kid who refused to grope the girls' breasts at breaktime—something that's (quite rightly) not in the least bit opportunistic or socially desirable now, post #MeToo, but is nonetheless true. Anyway, it was highly likely, I thought, that the young whippersnapper who dared to cut loose and challenge the general order of things, the rebel, would be the same guy who got all the chances with the girls. Undoubtably. Especially when I thought back to all the chances I myself had missed over the years by insisting on being way too sensitive, cautious—and chickenshit. At the same time, I argued (perhaps hoping to assuage the pain of this insight), at the end of the day it was best to be your authentic self. Any kind of role-play or charade would come out in the end, no? They would, wouldn't they? I had been raised to be nice and well behaved, and in many respects I lived up to the requirements imposed by (what I supposed was) my own social group—and, presumably, there wasn't all that much I could do about that.

Of course, Dream Maria—that perverse mutant or hybrid being—had nothing to do with the Maria of reality. I under-

---

[*]Larsson, S. (1983). *"Varför fick G så dålig kritik?"* ("Why Did G Get Such a Mauling?") *BLM: Bonniers Litterära Magasin* 52(5), pp. 348–351.

stood that completely. At the same time, it was hardly as though I was master or censor of my nocturnal dreams. When it came to Reality Maria, I never saw her as particularly mysterious, generally speaking. Not at all, really. Granted, she'd surprised me with the finger, but it wasn't like she'd violated my manliness in any way, of course not. At least not profoundly. Nor had she ever made any scandalous proposition to the tune of her possibly (on an appropriate occasion) wearing a strap-on (to, you know, spice up the sexual act), but perhaps that wasn't really her cup of tea, I supposed, and, to be frank, I'd never agree to anything like that either.

Anyway, Maria was now lying on the sofa in gray sweatpants and a T-shirt (with Hard Rock Cafe Lisboa emblazoned across it), listening to what I presumed was *Alex & Sigge* (or one of the other podcasts she liked) while scrolling her way through Instagram. Occasionally she would let out a chuckle—perhaps at a funny post, or something that Alex or Sigge had come out with. Something witty. I myself never normally listened to *Alex & Sigge*, so I didn't know the sorts of things they chin-wagged about. No doubt pretty mundane stuff. For all that, I did imagine they might sometimes go "deep and meaningful" in a way that I would find fundamentally moronic, and their fans would then spread these "wisdoms" like word viruses at watercoolers and dinner parties. "Alex actually said something really interesting a few days ago, about the relationship between father and son, *blah blah blah*," or some such like. I may have been wrong. But all those so-called writers who gave their books supercringey

Paulo Coelho–type titles in the hope of making them formidable *middle-aged-lady bait* almost scared me a bit.

I put my headphones on and pulled up SVT Play, only to suddenly be struck by an intense sense of déjà vu. Something about this situation, this *milieu*—me in the armchair with my laptop on my lap, Maria on the sofa with her iPad on her chest— felt extremely, indeed, even brutally familiar. Which it was. It was, in all likelihood, a completely and utterly, 100 percent run-of-the-mill situation in billions of people's banal everyday lives, wherever they were in the world. Two or perhaps more people in a living room, each one occupied or rather *consumed* by their electronic plaything, together and close to each other in a purely physical sense, but at the same time utterly alone. Did Maria need my physical presence in this room? Did I need hers?

No. We fundamentally didn't need each other, not in this situation, not till one of us started demanding something from the other. Sure, I could call out for Maria's attention at any time. But why? So that she could give me some sort of validation? I had no need for any such thing.

In any case not right then. I was, I thought, largely *satisfied*. That being said, I did entice Molly over, who'd been lying shakily at Maria's feet. The dog got up, jumped down from the sofa, pranced over to me, and jumped up onto my lap, and I genuinely noticed an immediate uptick in my mood. The little doggo was so touching in her stupid cuteness. Maria didn't even notice that Molly had abandoned her. Or, well, after a while she did stretch her legs out, which Molly's position had previously blocked.

The BBC's documentary series *The Planets* was tremendously ambitious and big budget. And very educational. It was from 2004, but the computer-generated images still held up well, I thought, or at least passably. Molly nudged me every now and then with her nose, and I absent-mindedly stroked the chronically shaky little thing.

"You would die *so . . .*" I said after a while with a snap of my fingers, "*so!* fast on Venus, Molly," since the episode I was watching was about that hostile, uninhabitable planet. I could just picture Molly screaming and jerking for a second or two, before going up in smoke or vaporizing completely. It then occurred to me that dogs probably don't really scream. Molly's doggy gaze followed the silver, computer-generated Soviet space probe as it passed across the screen. Maria, who was completely mesmerized by her tablet and what I assumed was *Alex & Sigge*, took no notice of us.

In the beginning everything was dust and gas, I thought while making a few subtle hand gestures (a bit like von Karajan conducting), and then it all—the whole enchilada, as it were—started forming planets and stars. We don't know exactly how that happened. Humanity will probably never find out.

In a way, I could understand Maria's peculiar (and perhaps typically feminine) phobia of space. It wasn't an affectation on her part; her fear was real. Those great planets were so huge it was beyond all human comprehension, beyond her phenomenological horizons. In addition, a black hole was a *black box* (in Bruno Latour's meaning): an inaccessible object in the cognitive sense, at least for your average folk. Black holes were of such incomprehensible and de facto *sublime* (or perhaps *numinous*) dimensions. The biggest black holes were also massive in an incomparably menacing and, I reasoned, almost *identity-crushing* way. Maria had very good (if not quite rational) reasons to feel abject terror and mortal dread when faced with the universe's *vastness*, *infinity*, and *magnificence*. Earth—which wasn't all that big compared to the gas giants—was protected, I learned from the program, by an atmosphere that extended just a few dozen kilometers above its surface. Apparently as thin as a layer of varnish on a billiard ball, relatively speaking. Indeed, even thinner, really. Anyway, I remembered astronomer Carl Sagan explaining it all on the TV series *Cosmos*, which I would never get Maria to watch. At a certain distance from the surface of the Earth, the air you breathed—if it could even be called air?—was like pure cyanide. You would die after just one breath. Besides which, the solar wind and Earth's electromagnetic field were locked in a constant and—thankfully— evenly matched battle, since without the latter the solar wind would have swept the atmosphere away and Earth would have suffered the same fate as Venus.

But why did I never take the piss out of Maria for her fear of space? Obviously the jokes would have more or less set themselves up. Well, I for my part despised the mere idea of *cannibalism*. I'd perhaps implicitly warned Maria about raising that topic, and she had in turn made it pretty clear to me that any space-related topics were a no go for her. It had entailed no great sacrifice, despite the great fascination I held for space. But then again, how often did people actually chat about gas giants like Jupiter and Saturn, Uranus and Neptune? And how often did the heinous topic of cannibalism ever crop up in conversation? When it came to the latter, the answer was—thankfully—seldom.

I couldn't hold out anymore. There was a cushion on my armchair, and I threw it at Maria's legs. Not all that hard, mind, but Molly barked disapprovingly. "What are you playing at?" Maria asked, pulling out her earphones. Well, it was kind of a beginning of a conversation, at least. To my surprise I had nothing to say in my defense. I'd just wanted to get her attention for a while, and now I had it. I shrugged and gave her a big smile. Maria yawned and shook her head as though I was an idiot, which I obviously was, in a way.

To be nice, I got up, walked over to her, and stroked her cheek, which she didn't care much for, so then I went and stood by the window and started rubbing one of the leaves of her money tree, while staring out at the café across the street and its outdoor seating area, which, as the heat wave had worn on, I'd noticed being frequented by an increasingly scantily clad clientele. It was chock-full, as per. Incidentally, when I'd fruitlessly stroked Maria's cheek, I'd noticed in passing that it was exactly as I'd suspected: she was getting her Instagram fashion fix.

The café I was now observing had been a frequent hangout of mine in my much younger days, back when I'd spent a few months—maybe even as many as six—staying in my older brother's flat on Risåsgatan, just a stone's throw from Linnégatan, after he'd gone off to university in Uppsala. The café had since changed name, and despite its proximity to Maria's place I hadn't been there in years. When I'd used to go there, there had been a woman working behind the counter who looked like she suffered from anorexia nervosa. And the other woman who sometimes worked there appeared to suffer from the same. Were they even alive now? I remembered them as extremely quiet and depressed, but perhaps that was just a retrospective fabrication.

Besides these extremely skinny, relatively young women—who were perhaps around twenty to twenty-five years old and as such several years my senior—I had two distinct memories from that café.

One day, two guys my age had come in who were possibly chatting in a broader dialect than mine and were also sporting caps (something that I at the time considered a clear or pretty much absolute marker of interests radically different from my own). I couldn't help but eavesdrop on the personal conversation they were having. One of the guys owned up to having hit his girlfriend in a fight, and from what he said I gathered that the girl had been mouthing off substantially more than him. He hadn't been able to get a word in edgeways, and in the end he'd flipped. "She wouldn't stop talking!" It was clear he regretted it a great deal. I don't remember what the other guy said, exactly, but he did try to console his friend. Despite the immorality of his actions, I felt a genuine compassion for the guy, but also a sort of envy. These guys might not have been particularly blessed with the art of eloquence, and they probably didn't go to Cinemateket to see cinema of the challenging European variety, either (otherwise I'd have seen them there), but on the other hand they did have girlfriends. I suppose even then I already had the impression that these, in my view, *simple* people—whose parents, contrary to my expectations, might well have been highly educated (despite their offspring's predilection for caps)—were more *alive* than I was. More *authentic* in some sense. In a *material* sense. Back then I still hadn't read Kinsey's observations in *Sexual Behavior in the Human Male*, about how middle-class guys—as well as deeply religious Protestants, Catholics, and Jews—made their sexual debuts considerably later than their working-class counterparts. Still, it was as though I'd known the score even then, that even half a century after the book was published it still held true (or still had *validity*, as they say). Yes, I had envied them, I remembered that much, but it wasn't something I understood at the time. There was so much that, for natural reasons, I hadn't grasped back then, I thought—things that now, some fifteen years later, I was nevertheless starting to gain a certain insight into.

The second memory concerned poetry. I had sat there—

most likely high on insomnia, as I often was in those days, and also filled with the paranoia that formed the flip side of youthful arrogance (and megalomania)—with a paperback of Tomas Tranströmer's collected poems, repeatedly reading and rereading "A Place in the Woods" from his 1978 collection *The Truth Barrier*. I don't know how many times I read it, but in any case the poem had hypnotized me completely. One or maybe even two hours had flown by in which all I'd done was read the same short poem over and over again. That being said, it's possible I also read "The Clearing," which featured in the same collection—or perhaps alternated between the two? (When not fresh in the mind the two are pretty easy to mix up, you see. I mean, they're like . . . well, like siblings in a way.) Anyway, something more or less magical had happened: in my mind's eye I'd seen gigantic trees soar up around me, like apparitions or shadows of trees that had perhaps once grown and stood in the very spot where I was sitting, where the café was situated, back before the inland Ice Age or maybe even further, hundreds of thousands of years, millions of years, or else like some kind of premonition, a sort of portent or presentiment of trees that would one day come to grow there, in the distant, distant future, when the houses on Linnégatan (where I now stood) or perhaps even the entire city had been pulverized by forces of nature, when humans had long since vanished from the face of the Earth and all trace of humanity been thoroughly wiped out. Truth be told, it had been a *mystical* experience, I thought, and, as I stood there by the window in Maria's flat, engaging in these rather melancholy reminiscences while gazing at the café that I'd once frequented and that had had a different name and where young women with anorexia had once worked, I couldn't quite recall ever having had as suggestive a reading experience since, at least not with poetry.

It would no doubt be something of a cliché on my part to claim that that particular Tranströmer experience had been the spark that lit the fuse, or some kind of origin story to me later getting two slender collections of poetry published (neither more than fifty pages) with a small Gothenburg publishing house, at the average debutant age of twenty-five years. (I had to pay half the printing costs myself, and they weren't reviewed in any of the major papers.)

But does anyone really know why certain people write po-etry? I asked myself and clasped my hands behind my back, as an even more distant memory washed over me: I was maybe five. My mother had given me some paper and crayons, and I'd decided to write *important letters* to all the neighbors on our terraced street. So I filled one A4 page after another with something that probably resembled handwriting in some shape or form. But since I was five years old and illiterate, what I'd actually written were illegible scrawls, like in Donald Duck cartoons when the irascible duck opens a newspaper, only to be riled by some article or so on—nothing but black wavy lines, completely unreadable, but with a clear reference nonetheless: *This is text.*

For me, these letters—their illegibility notwithstanding—were of inestimable value, and I suppose that's also why I could remember the immense happiness I'd felt as I stood on tiptoe to reach up to each one of my neighbors' letter boxes and share my most important, extremely valuable, and all-but-priceless epistles. Once I'd slotted one of them into each letter box there was no going back. The whole thing had been deeply satisfying; I remembered that now. I'd been completely convinced that my neighbors would be delighted, grateful, and even flattered.

Anyway, I thought, the whole thing had started with the imitation of something that I must have realized grown-ups valued—and perhaps that very same imitation and repetition of other people's behavior and habits was something that would never really stop. If I was (or was to become) a so-called man of letters in any shape or form, it had definitely started there, I thought, in a leafy residential street in Gothenburg in the early nineties, back when people still sent letters.

Suddenly it struck me that these reminiscences were quite possibly daft and narcissistic and most likely Knausgaard-influenced, so I gave a slight shudder and turned away theatrically. I had been so completely absorbed by my autobiographical ruminations that I hadn't noticed that Maria had pulled out her earphones, set her tablet down on the coffee table next to Coddington's *Grace*, curled up on her side, and gone to sleep.

This sweet sight filled me with tenderness.

I couldn't quite deny that, all things considered, she well and truly did possess certain masculine attributes and could even look like an *ephebe* with her sharp, makeup-less features and short, tousled, Twiggy-like hair. Molly was lying by her side with her eyes shut, but after a while she lifted her shaky head, jumped down onto the parquet, and padded over to me, apparently wanting something. I went into the kitchen with her, filled her bowl with dry feed, and watched her for a while. Immediately I noticed that she didn't appear to be eating with her usual zeal and gusto, so I started speculating as to whether it might be something to do with the heat. Perhaps we were supposed to get more salt down her, what with the weather being so hot? "Would you like a pinch of salt on your Frolic, Molly?" Yes, that was something I would put to Maria when she woke up. Perhaps we could give the poor thing a . . . uh, salt stone or something? Those things that hamsters have? It was kind of cute to see how sluggish and tuckered out the little thing was, but in the end I got tired myself, so I went and flopped across Maria's king-size bed.

5

A FALSE MEMORY OF THE ROYAL FAMILY'S PRESENCE

By mid-June the heat wave had mostly started to get on my and several of my colleagues' nerves, or in any case I'd started to suspect that the heat was affecting our collective mental functions to a degree that we, it struck me, perhaps weren't even necessarily fully aware of at the time. Me, I started my short working days early, so I had it pretty good when it came to the heat. That being said, I was having to run around between departments more than usual, but my tasks were also pretty simple, maybe even too simple and too few (which was possibly a contributing factor to my being considered dispensable and thus being one of the first to be given notice), and in those four morning hours I often managed to accomplish most of what needed doing that day: I would pore over the data records for a while; book travel and hotels where necessary; update the intranet; and comb newspapers for articles about accidents and emergencies and anything that could potentially be of interest to the Unit (the lengthy heat wave was not considered a trivial matter internally, no siree)—but by that point the full-time staff would be starting to get a strange look in their eyes. The building was sorely lacking in any modern, satisfactory air-conditioning, and the temperature could easily soar to 86 degrees wherever there was direct sunlight.

Since I often stuck around to eat lunch with my colleagues, I got to hear a lot about how the heat was affecting them. Especially Solveig (who was most likely menopausal)—she grumbled and moaned no end. I felt sorry for her. But Solveig wasn't the only one who was suffering in the heat. Lasse was really going to astounding extremes in his evolutionary biological speculations about the Nordic peoples' inadequate coping capacity for the intense weather—the blazing sun and oppressive heat, the horribly still air—but he was no doubt right in his comment that in the prevailing conditions it certainly made things easier if you had substantially more melanin in your skin; Jonna the clerk, who was a strawberry blonde (or, let's be honest, a ginger), said she would love to carry a black umbrella around with her for sun protection (à la Michael Jackson); the only thing holding her back, she said, was the fear of being made a laughingstock. Instead she used a cream with SPF 50. "It's likely to have serious consequences, this is," Claes had said, "above all for the old and infirm, as usual. Then there'll be drownings on the rise. It's *already started*, by the way. Of course people are going to be swimming more in this heat. After that, train disruptions due to tracks buckling in the heat. Forest fires. Maybe even emergency animal culls. There'll be a hell of a lot to assess once this is over."

"And they're only going to get more common, what with climate change," added Lasse, who was normally something of a climate skeptic. "The cities especially are of course already vulnerable to local weather phenomena."

Lasse, who was a few years older than me (and worked in infrastructure), also told me that one day he'd given in and started wearing shorts while pottering around in his garden, something he usually avoided as he was ashamed of his skinny legs. He said that his sister, who'd popped over to see him one day, had looked at him in shock—first at him, then his snow-white legs, then back up at him—before asking in alarm if he was sick.

"A gentleman never wears shorts in town," I said. "James Bond wouldn't ever wear shorts in a city—only on the beach."

"Oh, good grief, I wouldn't dare wear shorts in town," Lasse replied. "No way!"

Evidently Claes was no shorts person, either, and I definitely wasn't, even if I wished I was: that would probably be much more comfortable in the heat. Incidentally, at work it was a big no-no to be anything but appropriately attired. Lasse and I were probably the only ones among the male contingent who didn't wear dress shirts every day. Still, I always put on a blazer or jumper if I was in a T-shirt. It went without saying that shorts would be deemed way too informal, heat wave or no.

Another spicy upshot of the heat wave, psychologically, was that for a while I was very turned on by my colleague Camilla, who was in her early thirties and, I have to say, tremendously attractive. For some time in spring she'd been pretty down, having just broken up with her boyfriend (or was it the other way round?), but she'd dusted herself off and seemed to be back in the market for a new match; she'd been wearing progressively more revealing clothes, at least. Still, I did my best to give the impression of being completely indifferent (which I suppose I mostly was). #MeToo had brought with it something of a (probably much-needed) social revolution and had made everyone more aware of Man's historic sleaze. It was impossible not to start reflecting on one's own past behaviors, or contemplating how one *should* behave in the future to avoid getting stoned or hauled over the coals. At my workplace there weren't really any genuine *social justice warriors*, even if Solveig did have a tendency to harp on about the letches she'd crossed paths with in her long working life. But most people indulged her with these rants, since she had a good sense of humor and was highly competent, generally speaking. Plus we all realized that the heat (combined with the menopause) had made her considerably dumber than she was.

"You have to drink lots of water in this heat!" I'd once suggested (out of genuine concern), to which she replied: "But then I'll just sweat even more!" She'd quickly realized how daft this had sounded and had had a good laugh at herself. She really had been—as she herself admitted, *nota bene*—on the verge of a nervous breakdown in those desperate summer months.

Incidentally, one day I did have a long and very rewarding chat with Claes about the American Centers for Disease Control and Prevention (CDC) and their "Zombie Pandemic" campaign, which they had used to raise awareness of emergency preparedness among the general population. A successful campaign, my manager believed, since according to him the CDC's website had crashed from all the visits. Indeed, it had been a smart move, he acknowledged, to use the popular *zombie apocalypse* scenario in that way. But he was still skeptical about my own suggestion of running a similar campaign in Sweden.

"The US population's receptiveness to that particular type of propaganda is probably far greater than ours," he said, "maybe because they're the ones who created the zombie mythology from the start . . . You know, I remember when me and a few friends saw Romero's *Night of the Living Dead* back in the 1970s. I didn't think so much of the film—I don't watch *The Walking Dead*, either—but nowadays it's a classic that the Yanks probably view with pride. To some extent I guess you could say that pop culture *is* the Americans' culture?"

I could only agree, even if I still thought that the Swedish Civil Contingencies Agency, or MSB for short (with which the

Unit collaborated closely), ought to be able to do something significantly slicker than the CDC's informative graphic novel *Preparedness 101: Zombie Pandemic*. In contrast to Claes—who was born in the early sixties, after all—I rated the first few seasons (at least) of *The Walking Dead* pretty highly. Incidentally, it was Claes—or perhaps Lasse—who recommended Max Brooks's *The Zombie Survival Guide* to me, and also Herman Geijer's comparable Swedish book *Zombie Survival: Your Guide to the Apocalypse*, which was an educational take on the same concept and offered a bleak but fair outlook on Sweden's crisis and disaster preparedness; a great deal had been cut since the Cold War's heyday.

As Maria had no classes over summer, she had gone to Stockholm to spend two weeks with her parents and a friend who had a summer house on the archipelago. I don't quite recall what reason she gave for this getaway from Gothenburg and me, but I seem to remember her mentioning something about the need to nurture her relationships, or something along those lines. That was plenty good enough. Me, I had been formally introduced to her parents a few months before, when they had driven down from the capital. Because they were just stopping off here on their way to Lidköping, where Maria's mother, Therese, had grown up, they only stayed the one night in Gothenburg, and to avoid getting under Maria's feet they had taken up at the Elite Park Avenue.

When we met them outside the hotel "for the indulgent traveler," Maria had asked if they were going to stop at Kinnekulle mountain[*] as usual. "Yes, definitely!" Carl-Johan, her father, had replied.

Maria told me later that Kinnekulle was something of a sacred place for her parents. She had never found out why. Personally, I suspected that either she or her little brother had been conceived in some bush there in the nineties, or else that Kinnekulle generally exerted some sort of magical pull in its status of ancient cult site à la Stonehenge. Even Strindberg had a fixation on Kinnekulle and apparently believed that the over-thousand-foot-tall plateau was a wholly human-made construction. Not to mention the discoveries of the Österplana meteorites, beginning in 1987, which gave added oomph to the mountain's mystique. The fossils (ranging from 1 to 20 centimeters in size) were classed as the oldest meteorite findings on Earth at around 480 million years old.

We had taken Therese and Carl-Johan to see *The Distance*, an exhibition by Japanese artist Chiharu Shiota at the Gothenburg Museum of Art. I was already familiar with Shiota's work; her visual, bespoke installations involving miles upon miles of dyed yarn were all but made for social media. Art critic Birgitta Rubin had even said as much in her review in *Dagens Nyheter*. At the Venice Biennale in 2015, Shiota had hung thousands of

---

*A small mountain (elevation: 1,004 feet) on the southeast shore of Vänern, the largest lake in Sweden (and the European Union). Kinnekulle, I later learned, is home to a quarry that local optimists dub "the mini Grand Canyon."

keys from knotted, crisscrossing threads that extended from floor to ceiling. For the Gothenburg exhibition she had tied red yarn to chairs and created boat constructions from string, or "a hundred or so gossamer vessels, made of simple, black metal frames and knotted white yarn," as Anna Nittve put it in her review in *Svenska Dagbladet*. *Aftonbladet*'s Fredrik Svensk hadn't been convinced. Which may have had something to do with the contrived, politically correct link to migration that the museum had smugly chosen to proclaim in all their press pieces. Now, on the one hand, while Shiota herself had "emigrated" from Japan to Germany, that's to say from one developed country to another—the idea that the successful artist should thereby have some wider experience of what it meant to make the perilous voyage across the Mediterranean in a barely seaworthy boat, like some destitute person (with a lot of melanin in their skin) was tenuous to say the least. Nittve's more phenomenological review had offered almost no analysis of the artist's political motives.

Anyway, I remember that at some point I'd complained to Carl-Johan that so-called normal people were more or less uninterested in art criticism. For us, that's to say Carl-Johan and Therese, and Maria and myself, it lay in our class's interest to have a handle on certain things, to possess a certain measure of "cultural capital." Though it was, I lamented, quite possible that we were a dying breed.

Truth be told, taking Maria's parents to see *The Distance* had felt like something of a cliché. But it was satisfying, too.

Carl-Johan and Therese had style, I thought, and had they been completely uninterested in culture it would probably have been much harder for me to win them over. After all, I did have a pretty good grasp of these things, I thought. And besides, had they just been your average silver-spoon sailing types from posh Östermalm, I probably wouldn't have liked them all that much, either. And yeah, they were pretty great. Sophisticated. Carl-Johan had been the headmaster of a high school that was pretty much upper-class incarnate, and Therese, who was fifteen years his junior, still worked as some kind of middle manager at a bank.

They could be the perfect in-laws.

After the exhibition, they invited Maria and me for Arctic cod at Kometen restaurant, which had been sold by superstar restaurateur Leif Mannerström and brothers Christer and Ulf Johansson to local celebrity Per Ove Lundgren and his family just the year before. Carl-Johan was a tad disappointed that he wouldn't get to see Mannerström in the flesh, but he still seemed very pleased with Kometen's vibe.

At lunch we kept to cultural topics to begin with, and Therese recounted with a magnificent tone of voice that it was a tradition of theirs to read at least a few books by the winner of the Nobel Prize for Literature each year. They had very much enjoyed Ishiguro's *The Remains of the Day*, less so *Never Let Me Go*. They had been skeptical toward Svetlana Alexievich's work at first but had nevertheless capitulated before *The Unwomanly Face of War*. Therese said she normally went to

Hedengrens bookshop in Stureplan—a literary institution—for the prize announcement each year, and that she had felt more or less "cheated" when Dylan was awarded the prize in 2016.

I was a bit surprised by this, as I'd been under the impression that people of Carl-Johan's (and perhaps even Therese's) generation more or less idolized Bob Dylan. Yet instead they had taken that prize as a sign that something was perhaps amiss. Carl-Johan blamed it all on Sara Danius, the Swedish Academy's permanent secretary; he said he'd read in *Expressen* that Horace Engdahl—a former permanent secretary himself, no less—had described her as the worst the Academy had had since 1786.

Since Therese had long since tired of her husband's nigh-on manic aversion to Danius, a woman whom Therese presumably regarded as one of the few honorable people in the whole sorry Academy scandal, she turned demonstratively to Maria and asked her about the sort of things—feminine matters—that completely precluded any involvement from both Carl-Johan and me, and we could thus engage in an exchange of views between us men alone. Carl-Johan inquired about my writing and asked if I was still trying to write a novel or whatever it was. I answered in the affirmative, but when he pressed me on what it was about I felt compelled to say that I had to keep it a secret.

"A secret?"

"Yes, I don't usually say what I'm writing about," I replied, and for some reason I felt mildly ridiculous, especially since it could potentially sound like I was trying to paint myself as an old hand at writing, some kind of veteran, a seasoned wordsmith—which I definitely couldn't claim to be.

"Hmm. Yes, that does sound sensible. Sometimes you have to keep your cards close to your chest. Fact is, I myself had an idea for a short story, or perhaps a play, a while ago, or, well, it was actually several years ago . . . Anyway, I'd read a biography about Kurt Gödel, Rebecca Goldstein's *Incompleteness*, and was fascinated by all that with Gödel and Einstein—you do know who Gödel was, right?"

"Not particularly well. I can't say that I do."

"Well, he's regarded as the greatest logician since Aristotle, best known for his incompleteness theorems of 1931. Anyway. Well, I found it fascinating that Gödel and Einstein, who both emigrated to the USA and spent the rest of their lives at Princeton, would walk to and from their offices at the Institute for Advanced Study together. The physicist and the mathematician. To and from the office, perhaps in constant conversation, animated debates, these geniuses, year after year! What did they talk about? Well, I thought that could make for a good play, or perhaps something else. I even raised it with the drama teacher, Bengt, at my old school, who also thought it was a great idea. Incidentally, he, too, was confounded that no one else had written a play about Gödel and Einstein's daily walks to and from the Institute of Advanced Study at Princeton. But when I later gave some thought to what they would actually say to each other, these icons, I realized that, despite being somewhat well versed in both physics and mathematics myself, I didn't have the foggiest idea what they might have discussed."

Anyway, I had a lot on my mind just then. I was potentially going to be forced from my job as an administrative assistant at a workplace where I was happy, liked, and well regarded by my colleagues. It had been genuinely depressing to live in that uncertainty at first, but after a while I'd at least accepted how things stood.

If I'm honest, it was in this period that I arrived at an important insight, despite the heat wave's supposed negative impact on intellectual prowess. I might actually have arrived at it even earlier, I suppose, but it was in the weeks when Maria was staying with her parents that it well and truly took root within me. Really, it had all started when I read horror novelist Stephen King's autobiography *On Writing* for the third time. It was the only book of King's that I'd ever read cover to cover, as I usually didn't appreciate his graphomania or extravagant deftness, but this time I truly did feel like he was *speaking directly to me*. I realized I would have to be much more conscientious if I was ever going to get anywhere with the novel that I'd been putting off writing for years, despite very much wanting to have written one (especially after my poetry publications aroused no interest whatsoever), since the novel was undeniably the genre that bore the most weight in the literary world.

In *On Writing*, King describes so-called learned people as the *laziest* people around and says that if given half a chance they would happily drift till kingdom come without lifting a finger. I felt extremely touché—and wanted to do something about it. So, I theorized, I should base my own writing practices (or methods) on those of more experienced colleagues who had managed to be the opposite of lazy. King's own extremely strong (perhaps even Protestant) work ethic would actually be pretty tough to live up to; he writes ten pages or at least two thousand words a day, every day, all year round, even on Christmas Day and on July 4, otherwise known as Independence Day.

Another writer who inspired me to get down to writing (i.e., become a more *professional* writer) was (strangely enough) Swedish popular novelist Jan Guillou.

"You can't wait for inspiration," he'd once said in a podcast I'd listened to,[*] echoing what many other professional writers (within what French sociologist of literature Robert Escarpit termed "the popular circuit") often had a habit of saying, for one. I got the feeling that Guillou enjoyed imparting these truisms in his *malicious* way, but at the end of the day he was right!

Obviously you couldn't wait for inspiration to come knocking. "Writing is *work*," Guillou had said. *Yes, of course it is*, I thought. Guillou was right—too right! "You have to write daily, at fixed times," he'd also said, and so on and so forth. For a long,

---

*Hellman, C., & Larsson, S. (Hosts) (October 21, 2016). Jan Guillou (#17). *Cyril & Stig. I otakt med samtiden. (Cyril & Stig. Out of Step with the Times.)*

long time statements such as these had rung deeply unpleasant in my ears, but the penny had finally dropped. All these truisms were true. Unquestionably. Why had I been so unreceptive to these extremely sound pieces of advice for so long? I could have kicked myself.

In the podcast, Guillou also presented an entirely plausible *psychological* explanation for the infantile defiance and reluctance that I had previously felt: young and pretentious writers *in spe*—so to speak—with lofty ambitions of being a cut above the rest, in fact have a number of *delusions*, Guillou had claimed. They want to write "highbrow," "challenging" literature, or perhaps even be a "genius" like Nobel Prize winners J. M. G. Le Clézio or Alain Robbe-Grillet, for example. "A genius writes only when he's 'inspired,'" Guillou had said, imitating a conceited person who fed these very delusions.

Once again I felt like the direct target of these taunts was basically *me*. Yes, I felt EXTREMELY ATTACKED, especially seeing as I'd previously thought it was completely pointless to listen to good advice from "journalists-slash-writers" like Guillou. He claimed he'd given up on his own snobby dreams of being a brilliant writer in 1968. He'd had a light bulb moment. Writing introverted and completely impenetrable (albeit "sophisticated") literature like the cultish Robbe-Grillet, or navelgazing novels like Le Clézio, was no longer of the essence.

"How can I best disseminate my ideological ideas?" he had asked himself. "Well, by doing what crime-writing duo Sjöwall and Wahlöö do," he declared. "Yes, I'm just going to write in popular genres . . . and dump my youthful ambitions of being a writer of genius."

After that, Guillou had written the novel *Coq Rouge*—his first in a series of immensely popular espionage novels about the nobleman-slash-intelligence officer Carl Gustaf Gilbert Hamilton—which had allowed him to freely express his lefty ideals (which I assume were pretty important to him) while also reaching a very wide readership, something that—unsurprisingly—led to financial independence on his part. So basically, I realized I really needed to get a grip of these wholly basic, common-sense-type facts. I needed, like King and Guillou (or professional writers more generally), to see that it was especially savvy to work fixed hours, *daily*, and produce a certain number of pages (or characters) per day.

This is also why, the very day that Maria left for Stockholm, I decided that, as soon as I got home from work (after picking up Molly from doggy day care, that is), from one to five p.m., Monday to Sunday, I would park myself at my desk (or, rather, the kitchen table in Maria's apartment) and at exactly *thirteen hundred hours* (as I believe they say in the military) put my fingers to the keyboard. The fingers of my left hand would rest on the keys A, S, D, and F, those of the right on J, K, L and Ö, while my thumbs would hover over the outer extremities of the space bar. The key F *as in Foxtrot* and J *as in Juliette* were marked with small projections or protrusions in the plastic, intended to facilitate correct finger placement without having to look at the keyboard in question. Those who had mastered the art of touch-typing, I thought, were thus able to transcribe with a minimum of typos even when blindfolded, even when blind as an Eros or Lady Justice herself. At exactly *seventeen hundred hours* my hands would withdraw from the keyboard, thus concluding my work on the novel for the day. I told myself that from that day forward I would stick to this routine with *autistic* discipline, and I had absolutely no intention of having my phone on, or of doing research online; I would instead treat those writing sessions as unshakable—and sacred.

To spend four hours a day, every day, working on what would hopefully become a novel that both I and a decent publisher would one day want to publish—no, I suppose that wasn't exactly setting the bar all that high. Be that as it may, it made sense not to get too carried away. If I was too ambitious I probably wouldn't achieve my goals. One initial problem I faced was that I had no fucking clue what my novel was going to be about, but I reasoned that sooner or later some sort of *story* would have to emerge. I planned to observe the freewriting method during these sessions and was firmly resolved that, henceforth, I would sit as though *chained* to my keyboard between one and five *every day*. And, as it would turn out, it was so mindnumbingly dull to simply sit out those hours without writing anything at all that I would *always* write at least something, to stop myself from crumbling out of sheer boredom.

Incidentally, in those early days it was a plus to have Maria's tidy flat all to myself. I felt somehow *cleaner* at her place than mine. More grown-up, in a way. Her home, I reasoned, was like a more grown-up theatrical stage on which my chances of coming off as a distinguished and conscientious writer were far greater than in my own worn, albeit now decently clean, studio.

The turn-of-the-century building that Maria lived in was considerably grander than my own stumpy tenement block. I would open the door to its fine lobby and ascend the staircase flanked by tall marble walls and sense that this daily routine transformed me in some way; I assumed another role, achieved a new amplitude of normativity. It has to be said that at times I felt like a marauding burglar or the *sole survivor* of a global pandemic, wandering around a deceased stranger's well-kept middle-class home on the hunt for tinned goods. At the same time, Molly's presence lessened this sense of alienation, especially since I considered her a constant reminder of Maria's existence; I'm also prepared to admit that I thought the little dog might possibly have some sort of telepathic contact with her owner, which forced me to behave in as dignified and decorous manner as possible in spite of her absence.

The fact is, in those first days I wrote quite a lot about my flat, a flat I was kind of ashamed of when I compared it to Maria's—a genuinely negative feeling that was partly reinforced, I suspect, by Johannes's "Story of the Neighbor" and perhaps also by what Jordan B. Peterson discusses in his at times insanely boring, yet noteworthy (and well-written) book *12 Rules*. My own home was "a (basically) defective person's home," I thought Peterson might be capable of thinking, a veritable *man cave*. Maria's flat, by comparison, was a wonder of order and self-control. In any case, the Canadian psychologist wouldn't have been best pleased with me had he conducted an impromptu home visit. Indeed, the more I thought about it, the more I realized I clearly *was* the addressee of Peterson's *obvious* message; even if I hadn't thought so at first, I very much did belong to the target group that—due to subpar socialization (and perhaps an all-too-far-flung youthful hubris)—was in need of reminding of the strong correlation between a messy room and one's own "being," one's own "psyche"; and if I wanted to get my psyche in order, as Peterson suggested I did, then I would have to start with my flat, I realized, my very own shitty little studio, even though by that point I had the option of parasitizing the Order that Maria's flat—and by extension her normative being and psyche (or quite simply her *normieness*)—nevertheless offered.

When it came to my by now increasingly indiscreet fantasies or *idées fixes* about Maria as a *shemale*, however—that or a modern, androgynous hermaphrodite character in a kicker's Adidas uniform (or alternatively a Hitler Youth getup)—Peterson's *12 Rules* was no great help (if it really was "help" that I needed?). Jesus Christ. Still, it wasn't as though Maria's slightly boyish air, which had obviously become more pronounced since she'd cut her hair short that spring, actually bothered me, but her insinuation that it was only because she was "flat as a bloke" (not true, by the way) that I'd been in love, infatuated, or even interested in her from the start still hurt or pained me in a low-intensity kind of way, especially seeing as I'd actually started to suspect there might be something to it after all.

Anyway, I found a passage in *12 Rules* that encouraged me to be completely straight with myself (interesting word choice given the context, but still) when it came to my feelings about her androgynous appearance (in the chapter Rule 4: "Compare yourself to who you were yesterday, not to who someone else is today"):

> *Dare to be truthful. Dare to articulate yourself, and express (or at least become aware of) what would really justify your life. If you allowed your dark and unspoken desires for your partner, for example, to manifest themselves—if you were even willing to consider them—you might discover that they were not so dark, given the light of day. You might discover, instead, that you were just afraid and, so, pretending to be moral. [. . .] Are you sure that your partner would be unhappy if more of you rose to the surface?*

Indeed, on that day, an extremely sweaty Friday, as I meditated on these wise words it also struck me that it wasn't completely impossible, but rather extremely probable, that Maria was something of a *tease* when it came to what she knew about both her own androgyny and her attractiveness—her *sex ap-*

peal in short—so when I recapped the incident at the breakfast table that time—when Maria had brought up the fact that she didn't have "real" (i.e., *big*) breasts—I actually suspected that yours truly—so shocked had I been at the time—had possibly overlooked the fact that she might simply have been taking the piss, and/or hadn't been entirely truthful, *since she'd simply been taken aback by her own peculiar ambivalence vis-à-vis her own breast size*! That is, a topic she never typically touched on. Indeed, I guess it's true that by then I'd started to feel a budding *spite* toward her. *Why humiliate her boyfriend in that way? Why make those lousy insinuations?* It was beneath her.

I put *12 Rules* down on the bedside table and weighed up whether to watch the second series of *Better Call Saul* on Netflix or masturbate in Maria's king-size bed, and I was just about to get up and shut the bedroom door when I heard Molly come pitter-pattering across the parquet floor. She started barking merrily. By then she'd figured out that the best thing for her was to ride out the hottest hours of the day on the cool tiles below the kitchen table, and thanks to this strategy she'd become something of a new dog; her shaking had eased up a little and she was eating heartily again. I was almost proud of her. Suddenly I felt an urge to entertain her in some way. "Look at this, Molly!" I said, then grabbed Totoro and took him into the living room, where I kicked the shaggy rascal in the backside and sent him flying in a long arc over the parquet floor before he eventually landed headfirst on the radiator below the window. Molly shot off like a dart—I'd never seen her move so fast!—and instantly started biting and furiously shaking Totoro's little bundle until it came clean off. I cried out in panic and Molly froze on the spot, the bundle dangling from her mouth. It was hard to coax it out. "Drop, drop!" I said, and eventually she gave in. Upon inspecting the damage, I suspected that sewing the bundle back onto Totoro's paw would be beyond my capabilities. But I had options. I could say that Molly had ripped it off (which was true) and wait and see how Maria reacted, or I could take it to the cobbler on Andra Långgatan. *I mean, they can fix anything*, I thought. At the same time, it did hit me that it would be embarrassing to take something as weedy as a Japanese cuddly toy to the foreign gentleman there; he would look down on me, even if I came up with some moronic lie about "my daughter" being "really sad" that Totoro had "fallen apart" or something along those lines. I would seem totally weak and femme. So the first option seemed the best. Molly started barking at me. "Yeah yeah, it's all my fault, I know," I muttered. "My bad."

The next day I took Molly to my dad's to help him put a new SIM card in his router; he was a bit of a technophobe these days. He'd never met Molly before, and I thought the old man would probably like her. When we got there I found him in an unusually good mood, or at least not exaggerating his decrepitude to histrionic levels, as he usually tended to do.

As expected, he lit up when he caught sight of the cute little creature prancing shamelessly over to him as he sat in his armchair in the spartan living room of his two-bedroom flat in Örgryte. With a certain effort he bent down to pat her.

After I'd changed the SIM card—the new one worked straightaway—I asked him how he was planning on getting to the polling station for the elections that September, since he couldn't get around without his rollator walker anymore and needed help getting up and down the steps in his building. He thought my older brother could probably drive him on the day. But the elections were still a long way off, and it would probably sort itself out one way or the other. I mentioned that apparently some people were scared Sweden might go the same way as Hungary, which was what I'd read in *Svenska Dagbladet*, but Dad really didn't think it would go so far as that. But, sure, he admitted, things would probably get harder—a harsher climate. Me, I didn't really know what to believe. When Johannes and I had been at Plankan lately we'd met a lot of completely normal people—regular nine-to-fivers—who'd freely admitted that they were planning on voting for right-wing populists like the Sweden Democrats.

People were saying these things more openly, even those who, generally speaking, didn't come across as all that xenophobic by any means. They were clearly just "sick and tired" of Sweden's blue-eyed immigration policies and state activism, and of Sweden becoming an increasingly "fucked-up" country. Both my father and I agreed that they had some valid points there. The current government had simply upheld the immigration policies cobbled together by the Reinfeldt cabinet and the Green Party in 2011. During the 2015 refugee crisis, none of the other Swedish parliamentary parties had dared so much as breathe a word about limiting refugee numbers, for fear of playing into the hands of the Sweden Democrats. Some people seemed to think that political correctness had died in 2017. Personally, I thought that was unfair. The pathological virtue signalers and bleeding hearts of the population (a.k.a. the middle class) would never, ever admit that mass immigration posed any problems at all, and even if, against the odds, they ever did admit as much, in their eyes it would still never justify a stricter or simply "normal" European immigration policy.

After making coffee for us both, I remembered that I'd told myself to ask Dad if my grandparents really had had the framed portrait of the royal family hanging on their kitchen wall that I'd seemed to recall them having of late.

"No, not on your life!" Dad replied with a surprising harshness. "Pieter and Elsa were Communists, for crying out loud. That's partly why Pieter emigrated in the first place." My grandfather Pieter (who became a founder at the Götaverken ship works) had been from South Africa originally. Even so, I dug my heels in for a while—I was convinced my memory was right!

"Nope, you're wrong! Why would you think they'd have a photo of the *royal family* in their home? . . . That's very odd."

I cautiously explained that I'd fancied that Grandma Elsa, that is, his own mother, had, in spite of her own political leanings, perhaps developed a fondness for the royal family in her autumn years. As so many elderly women tend to do.

"No, not a chance! That's not how it was at all. I'd have *bust a gut* if I'd seen a photo like that in my parents' home! No, there were definitely no portraits of the king and queen on their walls. Absolutely not."

Truth be told, I was a little put out by my dad's categorical replies, as I could have sworn I clearly remembered seeing a portrait of the royal family in Pieter and Elsa's kitchen at some point. But according to Dad they were definitely no royalists, and it wasn't especially likely that he—their own son—would be wrong there. They did have a sense of humor, mind, Elsa especially, but they would never hang a portrait of the royal family for *ironic reasons*, not in prime position in their kitchen, alongside portraits of their own family. That would have been completely beyond the pale.

It wasn't like they were *postmodernists*, I thought. Besides, they were quite serious people at heart. Born in the 1920s, they belonged to a generation that had known true poverty: the Great Depression; the Second World War; the Cold War. They got caned in school. When I was little, I remember Elsa telling us how she would be made to hold out her hands for her teacher to lash her across the fingers with a wooden ruler. They were forced to drink castor oil; have their tonsils removed; and maybe even have their skulls measured in the name of eugenics.

After my question about the portrait of the royal family my dad had sized me up suspiciously for a while, as though he thought I'd compromised his parents' memory in some way. I personally liked the royal family, though I wouldn't openly call myself a royalist or anything, and so if Grandma Elsa had also had a soft spot for *these fine representatives of Sweden*, I'd thought, then, well, maybe it would have given my own quasi-royalist feelings some sort of legitimacy, too?

"I don't know where I got that from," I said in the end.

"Well, sometimes we misremember things, that's all," said Dad—and to my relief he seemed to give me a conciliatory smile, despite my royalist blunder.

"Oh, by the way, before I forget," he said chirpily. "You do know who Peter O'Toole was, right?"

"Jesus Christ, of course I do," I replied.

"A week or so ago I rewatched *Lawrence of Arabia* on SVT, and it reminded me that I had a book about him, the lead actor, Peter O'Toole. I think your brother might have given it to me as a present at some point, or I—"

"It could be my copy," I broke in.

"Yours? Oh yes, it could well be! Anyway . . . well, it wasn't just about O'Toole, but also . . . whatshisname . . . Richard Burton, and who was it now, another couple of British actors who enjoyed a tipple or two." (My dad was undoubtedly referring to Robert Sellers's *Hellraisers: The Life and Inebriated Times of Richard Burton, Richard Harris, Peter O'Toole, and Oliver Reed*, which I could clearly remember buying at London Heathrow roughly ten years prior, but which I guess I must have then left at his place for some reason.)

"I mean, more than one or two. They were massive alkies," I said.

"Yes, you can say that again. Anyway, I started reading it, or at least the parts about Peter O'Toole, since he was the one I was most interested in after watching *Lawrence*," said Dad, who then took an excessively long pause.

"Okay . . . so?" I eventually asked.

"Well, I must say it gave me some good belly laughs. Like when the author recounts how O'Toole and another actor who was also working in Ireland in the early sixties had sat in a pub all night, and in the end couldn't get served anymore since the pub had already called last orders. So they wrote a check and bought the entire pub . . . just so they could go on boozing!"

"Haha."

"Then they came back the next day and changed their minds. As luck would have it, the landlord hadn't cashed the check yet, so that was good. Haha. Apparently after that they became firm friends with the pub owner. So much so that when he passed away a few years later his wife invited them to his funeral. They both got down on their knees and were full-on bawling when his coffin was lowered into the grave, but as one might have guessed they were, as usual, a little the worse for wear, so to say—I mean, it's not unreasonable. Anyway, someone twigged that . . . well, something wasn't quite right. Maybe they were out of place in some way. Compared to the other mourners, that is. Turns out— haha—they were at the wrong funeral! The pub landlord's was going on one or maybe two hundred yards away!"

6

THE HOUELLEBECQ TEXT

The caption that graced the front of the postcard—and which was clearly a reference to Jack Nicholson's *As Good As It Gets* (just as the French author had suspected upon receiving it a week or so before)—read as follows:

"Whenever in doubt: F**k!"

The corresponding image showed a perhaps two- or three-year-old boy (judging by his blue cap and dungarees in the same shade) attempting to hug a little black pug from behind. Given the child's virtually blissful smile and the dog's at once surprised and slightly witless facial expression—combined with the aforementioned caption—it was evident that the first association the image was supposed to call to mind was the good old doggy style.

And yet the author of *The Elementary Particles* didn't consider the motif strikingly abhorrent; it was, after all, one of the least obscene or bizarre postcards that his seventy-year-old friend Iggy had sent him of late. In the field in which your average person would tend to write a bland and dispassionate message to the addressee, the pop star had scrawled the words: "*Go fuck yourself, Michelle!*" and nothing more.

Now the author used the postcard as a bookmark in Canadian psychologist Jordan B. Peterson's *12 Rules for Life: An Antidote to Chaos*; he placed it between the page with a drawing of a girl (holding a dog in her arms) and the first page of the twelfth chapter (with the rule: *Pet a cat when you encounter one on the street*). He put the book down on the sofa, took out a packet of cigarettes, and with some effort got to his feet (he had made it through almost the entire second half of the book in one unbroken sitting), then gently stamped his benumbed foot and cautiously walked over to the window overlooking the orbital highway out of town. There he thought—as he lit a cigarette some three hundred feet above street level in his apartment in Paris's Chinatown, Les Olympiades, the 13th arrondissement—that even though the points of contact between him and the Canadian psychologist weren't exactly obvious—no, certainly not!—it still seemed to him that they existed—of course.

The West could very well collapse as a result of what the unsuspected backlash against late capitalism had made of the citizen. *She* was now almost exclusively a *consumer*, and her *identity* as such—indeed, her *individualistic* consumer identity—remained, depressingly enough, what was most central, most imbued with symbolic value, in these rarefied marketplaces that had once been nation-states.

Humanity's sense of a shared purpose, a shared responsibility for its own existence, had gone up in smoke in the 1980s. There weren't even any guarantees that the Westerner—in her current, atomized form—would survive the present century, he argued. The individual- and ego-centric culture that had emerged in the metropolises of the Western World had spread like syphilis across the globe; the cement that had once held people together had been irrevocably lost.

Yes, we are probably doomed to annihilation.

The author of *Platform* recalled something that he had read: A *de facto* dramatic change had taken place in Western men's sperm over the past forty years; their sperm count had declined by roughly 50 percent between 1973 and 2011, on top of which the individual sperm were now also of poorer quality. Science could not yet fully explain the reason behind this deterioration in seminal fluid, but he personally suspected that the *psychological feminization* of the man had finally started to take its toll. One might even (like Peterson) suspect that the fact that, according to certain studies, heterosexual women had a preference for faces with less masculine features when they were taking the contraceptive pill could have led to the reproduction of increasingly feebler genes since the pill's invention in the 1950s. Especially given that the selection of a partner, the author reasoned, would not seldom have been made under the influence of the pill's tendency toward men with *less* testosterone. Over half a century of reproduction could thus have started to have statistical effects if the mothers of the Occident were indeed selecting increasingly weak partners with whom to procreate.

The biological or genetic adaptation to, or *correction* of, the average woman's "aesthetic" preference—not to mention to the phthalates in polymers, plastics and rubber, paint and glue et cetera (i.e., wholly environmental factors)—could take as long as twenty-five thousand years to occur, but until then . . . *indeed, we might well be done for before then*, he predicted.

Parenthetically, there were also other reasons why one might expect a slow suicide for the Western World (in particular): if humanity by and large couldn't find an outlet for its own need for closeness—in an *authentic* sense—then, ultimately, it probably wouldn't propagate itself. It wasn't unreasonable to expect that certain men would give up their sex life, he thought, while others would opt for voluntary sterilization; nor was it any great stretch to imagine that the internet—*YouPorn* and *Pornhub* and the like—and its inexhaustible offering would have the capacity to provide a not entirely unsatisfying substitute for real sexual relations.

And then there was always Thailand.

But, he reasoned further, certain men (and even womenfolk) were, regrettably, incurable idealists and masochists.

Their future prospects were bleak. The choice to have no off-spring would be a completely natural biological reaction to a world without love, without intimacy, without tenderness—in any case for anyone who wasn't a barbarian or a monster.

Humanity is starving . . . and the little slut's even enjoying it, he mumbled suddenly, almost taking even himself by surprise with the unexpected aggression of the remark—at least until he recalled the moment earlier that day when (diligently shadowed by security officers) he had stood fidgeting impatiently behind a young, martyrishly anorexic women in the checkout queue at Monoprix. He could clearly remember the contradictory feelings that the latter's *extremist* appearance had called forth within him.

The woman, that completely unfuckable, Madonna-like figure, had placed such strikingly, demonstratively meager, downright incomparably sad foodstuffs on the checkout belt.

The plump cashier (forty-plus), who presumably accepted the world in full and was in all probability quite capable of giving her man a passable blow job, had cast the woman a quick, shifty glance and then avoided eye contact completely. She had even lost her train of thought and forgotten to chirrup the now-standard "Have a nice day."

In that very moment it was, he thought, as though he had seen the anorexic creature and *furthermore also himself* in a sort of lightning-bolt luminosity; fully and completely he seemed to intuit a certain radioactivity in the narcissistic pleasure that the skeletal girl probably drew from this dreadful battle against her own nature; clearly and plainly he seemed to detect the contours of the euphoric sense of self-importance that her apparent control over her own suffering must have fashioned within her; her power, too, over her loved ones' despair, her parents' clearly *pathetic, abject* helplessness.

A miscalibrated, antisocial, and downright decadently feminine "desire for power," thought the author of *Whatever*. She was probably incapable of satisfying a man sexually. Perhaps even herself? Obviously she would kill herself if *she* wanted to, if *she* felt like it, for such was only fair, or so he imagined that she—this to him completely unknown child of misfortune—had thought, and it had well and truly looked as though that might have been the case. All too soon. All too late.

In other words, he really did feel very sorry for the little cow.

He couldn't bring himself to think anything else. But her radically narcissistic rage and violence—which he had for some seconds perceived as an existential threat to his own person (indeed, to the limits of his own *ego*), especially since her fanatical gaze, which had fleetingly met his own when he had loaded his own shopping (six bottles of wine) onto the belt—had extended so far beyond herself, spilling onto her fellow humans, contaminating, violating them.

In this respect the anemic young woman was hardly innocent, and she was certainly neither harmless nor powerless. A living death has no sisters, no brothers. Her war unto herself (and the world) probably afforded her some sort of mental reward, he speculated; a *chemical* (and in everyday talk unmentionable) gift. It was not unreasonable to suspect that she had become addicted to it, in the way that soldiers and war correspondents not infrequently became addicted to the constant stress of war (and the fraternity of their comrades-in-arms)—indeed, addicted, as it were, to the *combat life* itself (as Prussian anarchist Ernst Jünger might perhaps have put it).

For is it not the case that, when the fight-or-flight response is activated in the hypothalamus, the body releases endorphins, dopamine, and noradrenaline? he asked himself. Yes, without a doubt. The equivalent, in other words, of a large dose of CNS stimulants (MDMA, cocaine, amphetamine); a veritable groundswell of *jouissance.**

The French author stubbed out his cigarette in the glass ashtray on the windowsill and immediately lit another, struck by the thought that he himself and also other writers who had a partiality for what one might call the "transgressive" tradition (such as Céline) could in fact deliver an equivalent effect on the *hypothalamus* in their treatment of . . . well, *abject* subject matter. When one attempted to move beyond the *status quo* something occurred in the brain, thought Houellebecq, and endorphins,

---

*Michel Houellebecq was certainly no fan of Roland Barthes, Jaques Lacan, or the so-called *poststructuralists*, but it was hard to overlook the fact that the definition of the term *jouissance*—which in French could mean both *satisfaction* more generally as well as *sexual climax*—as an excessive and transgressive form of *pleasure* (associated with the "dissolution" or "fragmentation" of the subject) worked well in this context.

dopamine, and noradrenaline probably had a role to play in this suggestive "transfer," "shift," or "mental teleportation"—or, at the very least, he concluded, neurochemistry is in all likelihood an inextricable component of the charge generated by an *unfiltered approach* to literature.

The sensation of falling in one's sleep.

A young woman doesn't cut herself just because it hurts, he thought. *There is undoubtedly a pleasure to be found in the violence that one can inflict upon oneself.* But the violence that he had and would continue to inflict upon himself as an artist *in literary terms* would not affect himself alone. Especially not now that it seemed likely that he and his fiancée, Qianyum Lysis Li, would probably be getting married any day now; it was unavoidable.

Nietzsche's *modus operandi* of antisocial profligacy had doubtless affected more than just the philosopher himself; it had sent ... indeed, how to put it ... *ondulations à travers l'histoire* ... in both directions! Yes, truly. A mystical line of inquiry, he realized of course, but one that was not at all unreasonable. The anorexic good-for-nothing might very well have managed to persuade herself that her self-starvation *solely* and *exclusively* affected her, *obviously*, but her deadly self-mortification in actual fact extended considerably further than that (if, for obvious reasons, in not quite the same way as Nietzsche's philosophical fractiousness). Indeed, her "illness" touched far more people than just her very closest family and friends. But did she realize that herself?

Did she realize that she wounded everyone who was witness to her sadomasochistic suicide? Perhaps, generally speaking, she aroused as much loathing (or at least distaste) as she did pity? It was not impossible.

And yet it occurred to the author that there was in all likelihood something deeply amoral about the pleasure that he nonetheless indirectly drew from the young woman's suffering.

There was no doubt that Houellebecq had felt an intense revulsion vis-à-vis her fragile person. But while he in many respects relished controverting the puerilely sociological narrative to which an orthodox world of thought presumably ascribed her suffering, he was also faintly ashamed; how could he, *a de facto privileged pig (and one of Europe's most celebrated writers)*, draw such cocksure conclusions about this wretched woman's psyche without having so much as spoken or listened to her for a single second? *No, that was not how a stoic philosopher should behave!*

Anyway, thought the French author as he sat back down on his sofa and placed *12 Rules* on his lap, *anyway*. The premise of the Peterson argument had nevertheless been that there was something deeply destructive about what had become of Western society. Naturally he himself wanted to say that love no longer existed, that it had been completely obliterated *due to a cadre of highly materialistic reasons*. But the Canadian psychologist wasn't quite so pessimistic. There was love in Peterson's world.

For Peterson *logos* existed, and with it the hope of salvation from nihilism, at least on an individual plane. But even the Canadian regarded the condition of the Western World as more or less pathological. Its crisis was a grave one. Indeed, he even believed that the identity politics of the radical Left, or "neo-Marxist postmodernists," could ultimately lead to genocide. Just you wait.

Indeed, Houellebecq noted, his and Peterson's common denominators, the interferences in their respective *Weltanschauungs*, were definitely not nonexistent. *We should be able to meet up somewhere*, he thought, then immediately felt far too diplomatic and obliging. At the same time, he couldn't deny that obviously he had found *12 Rules* a pretty lowbrow or banal book. To read the work was truly no guilty pleasure—it was no pleasure at all; in fact, he felt a little ashamed at having slogged his way through it, though of course the wine did help.

As per, then.

Anyway, keeping à jour with intellectual trends in the Anglo-Saxon West is part of my duty, he persuaded himself, and if someone should happen to confront him on that point then that was exactly what he would say. Indeed, someone might perhaps ask: "But for heaven's sake, why read that charlatan? I thought more of you," to which he would reply: "I am duty bound to keep somewhat à jour with intellectual trends in the

Western World, including those pertaining to popular culture."

Peterson—a sort of internet phenomenon—wasn't "lowbrow," exactly, but then again . . . especially when it came to *12 Rules* . . . "middlebrow," perhaps. Behind the Canadian's obvious platitudes lay a certain substance that the world-renowned novelist could sympathize with, of that there was no doubt. Peterson's *rules* were only *superficially* banal. *Stand up straight with your shoulders back.* Unquestionably good advice, he thought. *Set your house in perfect order before you criticize the world.* Also good. *Do not bother children when they are skateboarding.* Perhaps less good.

Have I ever bothered a child when they were skateboarding? he asked himself. No, it had never happened. But that was obviously a metaphor, of course. Young men behave like idiots and must be allowed to behave like idiots (for such lies in their egomaniacal, narcissistic, adrenaline-charged natures). Only if they are lucky enough to survive the madness of puberty can they advance to the next level, that's to say the more sophisticated hellscape of the adult world.

And yes, Peterson was perhaps something of a quack. But then again: Couldn't one, generally speaking, regard all theology as quackery? Couldn't one in fact view Peterson as a sort of *Trojan horse*? he thought, inspired. Almost in the same way that Marxist sociologist Michel Clouscard had felt that the '68 movement, for all its Marxist hippie veneers, still bore all the hallmarks of your average libertarian social liberalism. *The Petersonian horse* would in turn serve as a *prophylactic* of Christian mysticism mixed with Stoic ethics, all while camouflaged as classic Western individualism, a cautious (liberal) conservatism.

While on the one hand Peterson the Kantian hero didn't offer entirely new paradigms, his thoughts were nevertheless so accessible as to appear revolutionary, in an age long since typified by liberal society's severe *anomie* and spiritual deflation. Hedonism had reached its limits, that much was undeniable. It was impossible to fuck one's way to a genuine experience of authenticity, competence, and true solidarity. Beauty's superficial worth was fleeting. Money and sex were . . . well, they were *good*, perhaps . . . thought Houellebecq . . . uh, to some extent . . . and one should reasonably be able to achieve mystically qualitative experiences with one's cock between a young woman's legs or in the mouth of a sixteen-year-old Thai whore.

This thought made the contentious author—not infrequently accused of cynicism—smile to himself. Though, of course, obviously . . . at the end of the day that was all just *pissing in the wind*.

He couldn't imagine Peterson being a so-called mindblowing fuck, not at all; the psychologist seemed all too overwrought for such an epithet, too much of a Boy Scout. Besides, he appeared to have been slavishly faithful to a woman he'd known since childhood; in their youth he and his wife had lived next door to each other in Edmonton, Alberta.

Besides, Peterson seriously cared about the *kids*, Houellebecq mused. That is, he *really* cared about lost young men. It was for their sake that he had created a religiously tinged or perhaps pseudo-religious text (or masses of texts, even, via YouTube and podcasts) that might have the potential to save at least some of the rich world's decadent offspring. Or was that too optimistic a thought? The psychologist might potentially even serve as a *worldview stabilizer* for a generation that had grown up and now started seriously pining for a more moral life-substance. Peterson's ethical concepts were no doubt already being spread around the globe, but it was unreasonable to expect such a Protestant *ethos* to be capable of unifying the culturally secularized world. *The opposite, more like!* thought Houellebecq and topped up his wineglass. Increased disunity could very well be the result—especially if Peterson was unable to admit his fundamentally *Christian* inclinations.

"The man's clearly Protestant. But does that really matter?" he asked himself while downing his glass in one. Perhaps not. Yet the crisis belonged to the Occident, and if Western Man was to survive then he would need a vigorous moral strategy. Absolutely.

When it came to the systems of economic and sexual differentiation, there was little to be done—money and sex would continue to play crucial roles in a ruthlessly social-hierarchical system—but it couldn't hurt humanity to give herself (or, rather, himself in this case) the chance to curb his own porn-surfing, his self-contempt and feminization, and consult the thinkers— Nietzsche, Jung, Eliade, Campbell, et al.—to whom Peterson, this perhaps excessively optimistic Pied Piper from Alberta, possibly served as a gateway. Even if Peterson was just a *useful idiot*, it was nevertheless too early to dismiss the possibility that his influence could have a far-reaching effect, especially if he became *mainstream* in a sufficiently widespread way. But wasn't that entirely dependent on how he would handle his celebrity?

Surely even an infinitesimal *metaphysical mutation* of Western Man via a pseudo-religious text (or series of pseudo-religious texts) was better than none at all? Or did so-called *memes* suffice? All in all, *12 Rules* was not the generic "self-help" book malicious rumor claimed that it was, he thought, running his hand almost tenderly across the light cover and glinting coppery title.

"No, it would be wrong to view it as such!" he cried out, as a freshly lit cigarette fell from the now-toothless author's mouth. Wasn't Peterson in fact the prophet the Western World deserved? he asked himself, nonchalantly fishing the fallen cigarette from between his legs. Indeed, was he not in fact perhaps the only prophet the West would tolerate? Was he not a didactic and pragmatic psychologist—a sort of carpenter of the soul—who wanted to give young men a *purpose* once again, confer an *intrinsic value* to their existence?

Take this yardstick, this *spirit level*, this plumb line—simple tools! Now adjust your inner architecture. Clean your room! *The room that is also you!* Yes, it's true, you'll probably still be a fucking loser, that's to be expected, but at least your mental illness probably won't escalate. Best case, you'll be a bit less of a cunt. Yes, you may perhaps even become a . . . more *dangerous* person, especially if you turn your back on liberalism's boundless tolerance and clinically doped-up openness. Chances are you'll even *have* to become a more dangerous person, my young friend, mark my words—unless you want to go under!

Houellebecq caught himself brandishing his fist like an old Commie agitator. *What on earth am I doing? Haha.* He shrugged and went on addressing his invisible audience out loud: "You must merge the *blond beast* with a Christian paradigm. How else will you ever compete with all those soulless animals?"

After chuckling at his own inspired waffle, he realized that the little book that he had been clutching parodically to his chest (as though it were Mao's Little Red one) wasn't seriously dangerous. It was no real knife, he reasoned, or. . . well, maybe a *butter knife*. But perhaps even a butter knife was better than nothing? Yes, indeed. *Fuck it!*

Houellebecq got up again with a sigh, and, noting that he was now pretty smashed, he made a beeline for the kitchen, on the hunt for some cold cuts and the day's third bottle of

Chablis. Before he got there he stopped dead on the threshold, when it hit him that there was a certain inherent paradox to this whole business of encouraging young men to dare to be dangerous—all while instructing them, you know, kind of like a generic "mum," to clean their rooms and make their beds. Haha! Yes, it did seem like a striking contradiction in terms, no? But Peterson was no positivist, he declared. Furthermore, surely one could be harmless and potentially very dangerous all at the same time? So long as the pin was never pulled from the hand grenade (a.k.a. one's self) then everyone else could just relax!

The incoming call on his mobile (no. 2) came from a withheld number, and it took the writer of the essay "H.P. Lovecraft: Against the World, Against Life" a few seconds to recall that he had a meeting scheduled that day with the police officer who oversaw his personal protection, and that it was highly likely he who was calling. Fact was, he had repressed all thought of that meeting. Which was strange, given that it was the entire reason why he hadn't gone to Marseille with Rex and Lysis to see that woman, Lysis's friend the dog acupuncturist. When he eventually took the call, he didn't recognize the male voice who informed him that he would be arriving at the author's apartment in around five minutes.

As the author felt caught off guard and quite drunk for this hour of day (around three p.m.), he replied with an overly loud and peevish "Looking forward to it!" before quickly hanging up, or, more accurately, snapping shut the flip phone that he had been supplied by *Direction Centrale du Renseignement Intérieur* (DCRI), who had wanted his communications with the authorities to be completely encrypted and totally "exclusive," as they put it.

The purpose of the meeting was to conduct a threat assessment ahead of the release of the novel that the author was to publish in the New Year. Since *Charlie Hebdo*[*] he had been compelled to—in all likelihood on the direct orders of the then–minister of the interior, Bernard Cazeneuve, and later his successor—submit to a not-insignificant security detail, the scope of which not even he himself was aware of; he had body-guards on constant rotation, and there was many a time when he didn't even notice them, especially when he was staying at home, which was what he now preferred to do.

Hmm, he thought, *I'm really way too drunk to discuss such serious things, but never mind!* After the doorbell had eventually rung and he had established that the person on the inter-com screen, which was linked to the security cameras outside the street door and in the corridor, was a suited-and-booted man holding his police ID up to the camera lens, Houellebecq let in a police officer of perhaps thirty years old (surprisingly young, in his view), who introduced himself as Police Inspector

---

[*]The terror attack on satirical magazine *Charlie Hebdo* in Paris, January 7, 2015.

Antoine Grayson. The author was slightly thrown, as he usually received the information, or *disinformation* as the case may have been, from another man, but Inspector Grayson, who appeared to have taken no offense at the author's peculiar tone in their short phone exchange, informed him that Superintendent Descamps had been admitted to Hôpital Cochin for an urgent appendectomy, and the younger colleague had had to step in for his superior at the last minute.

"Only temporarily, though," he declared, adjusting his light-blue silk tie.

"Well, that's *no problemo* for me," Houellebecq said with a servile politesse (possibly to compensate for his inebriation). He was struck by how surprisingly well dressed the inspector was for a pig, but imagined that his dad was perhaps a commissioner or something similar, and, after sizing him up, he went on: "It's nice to see a new face every now and then! . . . Shall we take a seat in the kitchen . . ." Houellebecq said and gestured toward the kitchen island, then back at the coffee table in his *master living room* ". . . or the living room, perhaps?"

"Which do you think is best, monsieur?"

"The living room."

Grayson sat down on a white Barcelona chair with his back to the panoramic window and congratulated the author, who had taken a seat on the sofa opposite, on his engagement to Lysis. The author gave an embarrassed, scarcely audible mumble in reply, along the lines of how he was a lucky man and his thirty-four-years-younger fiancée was a formidable woman.

"We'll probably get married in autumn," he whispered laconically.

After being offered a glass of wine—which he refused—the inspector got straight to business:

"So, what sort of themes are we looking at for your new novel? Should we have reason to believe that . . . uh, there's any chance a certain 'demographic' might 'go off' about anything in particular?"

"You are, I suppose, referring to Muslims, or rather Islamists, are you not?" Houellebecq asked without looking at his guest, then went on without waiting for a response: "I doubt there'll be any issues this time round. None at all, I should think. Briefly, it's about a middle-aged man by the name of Florent-Claude Labrouste, who one day discovers his Japanese girlfriend is a depraved dog-fucker. He gets depressed, as well one might, I imagine, upon learning one's partner engages in bestiality. He ends things, of course, and starts taking a new SSRI medication that makes him fat and impotent . . . and, well, perhaps gives him a full-on personality disorder, or what have you."

The author fell silent, shut his eyes, and nodded for a few seconds.

"And then? . . . Or is that it?"

"Ah! Yes, sorry, no, then . . . then he runs off to stay with a friend in the countryside, where he witnesses how Brussels is driving farmers to the brink of suicide. But his aristocratic comrade and the farmers give Brussels a taste of its own medicine, and it all ends in a . . . well, *bloody* confrontation. But otherwise nothing out of the ordinary. In any case nothing remarkable. Some German feathers may be ruffled by a Germanic pedophile who makes a brief appearance, but the German people—or ethnic Teutons, to be exact—don't tend to be any problem at all nowadays, generally speaking—at least not when it comes to terrorism, so to speak . . . Do you read much?"

Grayson seemed thrown off by the question.

"Literature? Yes, I read a fair bit."

"It's good to read," said Houellebecq, who then visibly shuddered and took a swig of Chablis.

"Yes, well, I expect it is."

"Very good, very good," said Houellebecq, who was in fact anything but convinced that he was right.

"But, just to be completely overexplicit . . ." Inspector Grayson said, then leaned in over the coffee table and asked: "You're telling me the work contains no . . . uh, how to say . . . *serious provocations*, as you see it?"

Houellebecq couldn't help but laugh; Grayson was clearly a *rookie*—that or he was simply pretending to be one, but either way the author liked the guy.

"Well, of course it's filled with . . . well, masses of provocative shit, as usual! But no, it doesn't contain anything that . . . uh, as it were . . . isn't already part of my *repertoire*. If you'd like to read it before it's published, be my guest. I might very well be blind to any substantial 'triggers' so to speak. But if so I'll expect you to keep the story under wraps. Though I suppose that shouldn't be particularly hard for you, should it?"

"No, indeed, the content we would certainly keep to ourselves . . . If it's all as you say then I shouldn't think we have anything to worry about. Besides the usual consequences of mass media coverage."

"Yes, it will attract some attention. I write that the EU's murdering France. This very second! The Western World is a dying culture."

"Dying?"

"Yes, actually dying. *Fucked.*"

"That sounds very bleak."

"It *is* very bleak, Monsieur Grayson, but it will happen, perfectly . . . well, perfectly quietly and calmly and . . . uh, *with no great fuss.*"

"Yes, it would be interesting to read the work," the inspector replied drily, then pulled out his notepad and wrote something down (which Houellebecq guessed was "EU murdering Europe?").

Having spent fifteen or twenty minutes completing his *debrief* with Houellebecq on how satisfied the latter was with his security detail in recent months, Inspector Grayson cleared his throat, adopting a manner that to the author verged on the comically officious.

"So, to summarize, based on what you've said: as I see it, we on the State's part are simply to expand our 'invisible' presence from now on, *precisely as planned*. This is, I should think, probably all that I can say. But I shall certainly get in touch with Descamps as soon as he's well again to hear his thoughts. After all, he is my superior . . . and has long been my . . . well, you could probably call him my *mentor*."

"Yes, he's a good chap, Descamps!"

The inspector nodded eagerly in response.

"Yes, he really is."

"Send him my greetings, won't you?"

"Definitely."

"Oh, it's just occurred to me that I should possibly even send him . . . well, some sort of bouquet, perhaps?" said Houellebecq, wafting a pantomime bouquet around in his hands.

"I'm sure he'd appreciate that."

"Men . . . men in general might possibly take things like flowers as a bit *gay*?"

"Uh, well, possibly . . . but perhaps not *all* men and perhaps not so much nowadays?"

"No, exactly . . . Yes, I . . . I'm probably exaggerating. But no, wait, wait! Flowers are *haram* in hospitals nowadays. Due to allergies and the like. I'd forgotten that. I'll send him a bottle of whiskey instead!"

"Yes, that sounds like an even better idea, if possible," Grayson replied with a sincere smile, before going on in a much more relaxed, enthusiastic tone: "The thing is, you see, I've read several of your novels. I very much liked *The Map and the Territory*. Not that I know all that much about the art world and all that, but . . . well, it was very thought-provoking . . . It must have been awful to write about yourself like that? I mean, you know, the brutal murder of . . . uh, *you* . . . in the book."

"Oh, not at all, it was more refreshing, if anything. A sort of exorcism, I should think. Sometimes I envisage . . . for reasons you may appreciate . . . a violent death for myself, à la Julius Caesar or Gaddafi. But one shouldn't hold back! . . . To attempt to die with anything even . . . resembling dignity in such a *situation* . . . indeed, I think one might potentially miss out on a more or less ecstatic experience by not truly letting go in such a *situation*, the last *situation* one will ever encounter . . . Perhaps it would resemble a . . . well, a cosmic . . . orgasm . . . or that's what I'm hoping, at least. Well, I mean . . . after *Charlie Hebdo* and all that, you know . . ."

Houellebecq paused and summoned all of his inner strength to see off a wave of discomfort, but still wasn't able to stop an agonized grimace from spreading across his haggard and increasingly Baudelairian face. The relatively young Inspector Grayson was unsure how to react, but correctly inferred that in his palpable state of drunkenness the author would be receptive to a *comforting* tone of voice.

"In any case, it's clear that you did a lot of research! On both art and . . . well, *the rest*. Thankfully the sort of crime you describe is rare. Extremely rare! Besides, with the protection you have . . . Indeed, the probability is extremely small that anyone could . . . well, so much as lay a finger on you. I mean, Jesus . . . I probably shouldn't say this, but . . . you don't *need* to worry. Put it this way: you're as safe as Macron."

"Research?" the author asked drowsily; he really hadn't been listening. "Yes, I had to learn a whole lot about police work, of course! That was really exciting. I also got some very nice help from that woman, Teresa Cremisi, and Principal Private Secretary Moreau and Police Commander Dieppois at Quai des Orfèvres. Otherwise it wouldn't have come off. Definitely not. I thank them at the end of the book . . . Are you sure you won't have a glass?"

"Well, perhaps now that the important matters are settled I . . . yes, why not! I'd love a glass of white, please."

"Certainly! I'll fetch you a glass," said the author, then got up and staggered off into the kitchen.

Inspector Grayson, who had actually read every one of Houellebecq's novels, suddenly thought about how the author almost always held his cigarette in an affected manner, between his middle and ring fingers. Like a bizarre dandy. This trait had become something of a trademark for the author. In the film *The Kidnapping of Michel Houellebecq*, which Grayson had seen with a few colleagues, the author had explained it away by the fact that he'd broken his finger as a child. As Grayson waited for the author and the wine, he remembered how some of the other analysts had speculated as to what this accident might have involved more specifically, that is, purely technically. A reduced strength in his index or middle finger could perhaps make it nigh-on impossible to hold a cigarette normally, one of them had argued, that is, without the constant risk of dropping it.

In the end someone had put forward the hypothesis that it

was perhaps all a gimmick, pure *show*, and that the old alkie was just putting on airs. Grayson, however, had contested that assumption passionately; inwardly he viewed the renowned author as something of a hero.

When Houellebecq returned from the kitchen he noticed that the inspector had placed his business card on the coffee table. It said:

Ministère de l'Intérieur
Antoine Richard Grayson, Inspecteur

"So that's how your name is spelled?" exclaimed the author of *Submission*. "Your name's *Richard Grayson*?" he went on with genuine interest, while filling the inspector's glass with an especially generous amount.

"Yes, what about it?" his guest asked, perplexed.

"Well, obviously I'm not saying that . . . you know, I'm not saying it's an *odd* name by any stretch. But it just struck me that you have the same name as Batman's protégé, uh, the same name as Batman's . . . what's the word . . . *sidekick*."

"Oh, yes, Robin! Yes, that's right!" said Grayson, suddenly seeing what he was getting at. "You wouldn't be the first to notice the connection. My grandfather was an Englishman. Of course, the name's more common in the UK."

"Well, I only mention it because a few days ago I was talking to a female acquaintance of mine who writes about pop culture for *Les Inrockuptibles*. She wouldn't stop going on about this theory she has about the caped crusader. She's kind of an expert on comics. A real nerd, I'd go so far as to say.

"Anyway, she said that an interpretation that some American psychologist did of Batman and Robin's relationship—in a book[*] that came out in the fifties—*sexualized* the public image of those characters [Houellebecq took a big glug of wine], because he believed the comic's creators had intentionally depicted them in a homoerotic light. Sabine—that's her name—felt that a reading like that would never have caught on had it not been sanctioned by someone belonging to the psychological establishment of the day."

"Yes, that could be true," said the inspector a touch nervously.

"In Sabine's view, he—this . . . Wertham, I think his name was . . . if I remember correctly . . . well, Wertham had described Batman and Robin's life up in Bruce Wayne's castle as some idyllic homosexual relationship, complete with a butler and perhaps pajama parties and all that."

"But is it really reasonable to read such things into a comic primarily aimed at *young* people?" Grayson asked, with a tone that struck Houellebecq as rather old-fashioned.

"Yes, that's precisely what Sabine was saying. The very effect of his, so to say, basically *anti-gay* book was *counterproductive*.

---

[*]Wertham, F. (1954). *Seduction of the Innocent: The Influence of Comic Books on Today's Youth*. Rinehart & Company.

Especially given that homosexuality was clearly an issue to Wertham. It had a *backlash*, as it were. In the sixties, Hollywood's image of Batman and Robin had been so influenced by his homoerotic take that the Adam West TV series was excessively campy in a way it absolutely wouldn't have been had Wertham not gayed it up so much in his book."

"I haven't seen that series," Grayson said curtly, giving the author the impression that he found the topic unpleasant, possibly because men of his generation—indeed, perhaps even pigs—were increasingly sensitive to anything that bore a whiff of "homophobia."

"You're not missing anything," replied Houellebecq, who was beginning to see he had perhaps overstepped the mark; for obvious reasons he couldn't know whether Grayson, who wore a wedding ring, might actually be with a man, however unlikely that seemed. "The series was on TV when I was young," the author went on. "But I never saw what the big deal was. Perhaps I was too old, perhaps too young. The TV screen was filled with words like 'BLAFF,' 'POW,' and 'BANG,' which appeared whenever the half-wits got into a fight with the villains. According to Sabine, Wertham took aim at Wonder Woman, too. Clearly she would have an adverse effect on young girls. They could probably be turned into man-hating lesbians or little . . . what's it called . . . *muff divers*. A wonderful turn of phrase. In short, a bad role model. Still, for natural reasons I'd take Wonder Woman over the flying rat and his little friend any day."

Houellebecq lit another cigarette, pleased that Grayson once again appeared to be enjoying his company.

"Come to think of it, there is, for that matter, an element of so-called *bondage* in those comics," he went on. "They were tying each other up endlessly. Endlessly. Hmm."

"Have you seen the film? *Wonder Woman* the film, I mean," Grayson asked.

"Yes, part of it, I think. Did you like it?"

"No, I probably preferred *Iron Man*."

"Yes, personally I wasn't all that enthused. Presumably it's a 'chick flick' though, no? More of a chick flick, in any case. I suppose those films generally, the Marvel films I mean, are pretty much just cryptofascistic propaganda. Not that they're any the worse for it. Not in my view. By the way, do you know of Jordan B. Peterson, the Canadian psychologist?"

Grayson looked at the author questioningly.

"Peterson? No, I'm afraid I don't."

"I've actually been thinking of writing something about Peterson. Perhaps a sort of satire. But he doesn't seem to be famous enough in this country. No one knows who he is. So I suspect there's no point writing about him . . . Come to think of it, Peterson's just a *Protestant* demagogue. It probably won't even matter if he's translated into French or not. Had he been Catholic and French-Canadian that would be another matter entirely, but . . . indeed, that would be a complete paradox. Surely it would be impossible for such a fidgety character to emerge from any French-speaking soil."

7

THE DUNNING-KRUGER EFFECT

I'd barely had a chance to take a seat before I was served a pint by Hedda, who for highly logical reasons now viewed me as a Plankan regular. "Still a free agent?" she asked me with a titter.

"Yeah, but Maria's back tomorrow."

"All the more reason to live it up a little tonight, then!"

Molly was assigned a metal bowl of water, lapped up a few hundred mils, and then eagerly pressed her little dog body to the stone floor to cool off, just like under the kitchen table back at Maria's place.

Originally my plans for that Saturday afternoon had been for us to walk from Linnégatan to the pub in Majorna, where Johannes and I had agreed to meet at four, but when I realized what a scorcher it was, I'd instead chosen to take the tram two stops from Järntorget to Stigbergstorget. Molly had actually been bright-eyed and bushy-tailed when we'd left Maria's flat, a veritable *trooper*, but I had the feeling she'd probably wilt pretty promptly in the heat, even if I did carry her some of the way; the tarmac was so hot it seemed wise to bear in mind that little dog paws, unlike the soles of my own shoes, were not made of raw rubber.

After taking my first swig of beer, which undeniably tasted very good in the near-saunalike establishment, I couldn't help but ponder the risks of drinking in the heat. When I'd chatted to Johannes on the phone earlier that day, he'd told me that the pubs along Andra Långgatan had been rammed by as early as lunchtime the previous day (Friday); hordes of guy groups with slicked-back hair and polo shirts had been "crabwalking" down the street in the sunshine, drunk as skunks—happy, one might think—and their faces completely red.

Indeed, I suppose the heat had quite simply been something of a "shock therapy" for the whole nation. Of my colleagues, Solveig hadn't been the only one behaving oddly of late, at the office on Södra Hamngatan where—ironically enough—we just so happened to be working on action plans to reduce the heat wave's negative impact on health. At least three people had called in sick, and Lasse hadn't even shown up in days. Claes—who, on the advice of the Public Health Agency and the MSB, had initiated Action Plan Ra (after the Egyptian sun god)—had made no bones of his displeasure at Lasse's and the others' bunking. As a matter of fact, Claes wasn't exactly his usual self, either. Action Plan Ra gave him "extraordinary powers," powers not even he regarded as entirely democratic. At times he seemed to want to play it all down, but it was clear that his increased authority had changed his personality. He went outside to (stress) smoke all the more, and he seemed completely obsessed with the data coming in in the daily reports from the Meteorological and Hydrological Institute and Sahlgrenska University Hospital.

Suddenly it hit me how extremely quickly I was downing my beer. It seemed like I'd only just gotten it, and the next second it was practically gone. Perhaps I was considerably more nervous ahead of Johannes's verdict on my "Houellebecq Text" than I was actually prepared to admit? (Wasn't that also precisely why I'd turned up at Plankan one hour ahead of the arranged time? To dampen my nerves with a beer or two?) As I may have mentioned, in recent days, or at least since Maria had made off for Stockholm to visit her parents in Östermalm and a friend on the archipelago, I'd been pretty productive. I'd managed to write at least an okay three-four-five pages per day. A material of distinctly varying quality, to be sure, but, as I saw it, I'd achieved something of an apex in my "Houellebecq Text" (in which Houellebecq kind of sits around in his apartment in one of the brutalist skyscrapers of Paris's Chinatown in the 13th arrondissement and wonders whether *maybe, just maybe, he might be* able to write something interesting about Jordan B. Peterson, whose *12 Rules* he has just finished reading). No, there was no denying I was nervous. As soon as I'd emailed the text to Johannes a few days before, I'd started properly doubting myself and my writing—indeed, even the meaning of literature as a whole.

Anyway, I drained my glass, gestured for another beer, and instead started speculating on the bizarrely persistent heat in more anthropological terms. Sweden probably was and is, I reasoned, by and large a country plagued by cold and darkness, sadness and melancholy. Swedes were naturally starved of sunshine and heat. So when temperatures in spring or summer suddenly soared—if you were lucky—to the low eighties in the shade, even the most unsophisticated or downright grotty restaurant terrace started to seem enchantingly, seductively enticing. To then have the chance to disappear into alcohol's veils of mist while accompanied by the sun's carefree rays undoubtedly offered a pretty irresistible break from the norm after months of vitamin D deficiency and depression. But that particular summer's hysterically good weather could, as previously suggested, also be a trap for the pale Nordic dweller. Drinking in the sunshine could undoubtedly lead to heatstroke, which was likely why people in Europe's sunnier climes didn't tend to drink in direct sunlight, I philosophized, unless, that is, they drank *exactly* the right amount in the sun? No massive benders in any case. Not when the sun was at its peak.

But when—as now—it started to get injuriously hot, 95 degrees, day after day, week after week, and you couldn't really classify the weather as "nice" anymore, those more familiar problems were replaced by other, far more profound and *mood-altering* effects. I mean, I myself had been mighty taken aback that my colleagues were as . . . well, as kind of *transformed* as they had been, though I myself, it had to be noted, was not at all immune.

For my part, I felt that the heat was increasingly flinging me into something that could practically be described as momentary flare-ups of totally pathetic sexual fantasies that I normally wouldn't consider my bag. While the 70- to 80-degree or more "normal" summer heat did perhaps increase the need for sensuality to some degree—or at least somehow relieved people from their ordinary *inhibitions*—the 96-degree, almost unreal and abnormal heat was appreciably more aggressive in its effects. It was as though whatever I laid my eyes on was contaminated with an almost obscenely glossy varnish, a perverse patina—a feeling that I for some reason associated with the erotic charge in Spike Lee's early works, films in which the actors often glistened with sweat and were not infrequently freshly fucked and, so to say, "exotic" in their look.

On a number of occasions I had recently—while, for example, sitting in an outdoor café or a beer garden with a view of unsuspecting passersby—caught myself fantasizing about literally throwing myself at the feet of the first passable (though preferably young, tall, and slim) bare legs that came within reach and licking them like a depraved prince in Pasolini's *Salò*. Whether these (ideally athletic) legs in fact belonged to a spotty young lad or a toned woman in denim cutoffs would probably be all the same to me.

In my defense, these probably weren't willful—or even fully conscious—fantasies on my part, but rather sort of momentary *flashes* of a depraved ilk, like little obscene pop-ups that suddenly appeared in my brain.

One person who was making all the more cameos in my more or less *boneheaded* 90-degree flashes was Camilla—that is, my colleague at the Unit—who, as previously mentioned, had over the course of the heat wave started seriously flouting the workplace's conservative dress code, primarily by wearing ever-flimsier blouses with no bra. Perhaps she saw the situation as tantamount to extenuating circumstances (which, at the end of the day, the activation of Action Plan Ra did affirm); no one had ever experienced a heat wave like it (and it no longer felt unreasonable to imagine that there was something well and truly fucked-up with Earth's climate). While one could reasonably assume that Camilla was wanting to signal that she was a fertile young woman on the hunt for a mate, in reality she was probably just as foggy as all the rest of us. Still, it was true that the heat had temporarily blown her sense of decorum out of the water. Obviously Claes had no possible way of intervening. Had he given Camilla even the slightest reprimand for her crimes against the workplace's unspoken dress code—had he so much as hinted at what he found unsuitable about her revealing wardrobe—he would basically just seem like a deeply unwholesome #MeToo letch. But, truth be told, I suppose Camilla exposing more bust than usual in those extraordinary days wasn't such an issue, really. Sooner or later she would sober up, one would assume; sooner or later everything would go back to normal.

Speaking of dress code, the twentyish-year-old waitress, Lydia, was bustling around in white, possibly almost too-short cutoffs, even though just a few days before I'd happened to overhear her being told by her boss, Hedda, who could have been twice her age, that Plankan's dress code was black or at least dark trousers during working hours. Something about which Lydia, respectfully, couldn't give a shit. Clearly. I understood her. Though personally I couldn't bring myself to wear anything but my black jeans, no matter what the temperature was, I completely understood that, so to say, normal people—who *didn't* have a complex about their spindly legs—felt it was way, way too hot to be in trousers.

Anyway. After dedicating almost an hour's wait to this everyday philosophizing, and with almost two whole pints under my belt, I was feeling considerably calmer than before, and I had genuinely started to look forward to hearing what Johannes had to say about my modest travails, this sketch—embryo, even—of something that could potentially become something bigger, and I suspect that was why my heart skipped a beat with pure joy and gleeful anticipation when I saw Johannes approaching through the doorway, saw this intellectual rock in my life come plodding down the street toward the pub across the searing-hot tarmac, a tarmac whose surface, just a dozen or so meters behind him, appeared to be coated in water, where the layer of hot air refracted the light to reflect the bright-blue summer sky; a so-called inferior mirage; an illusion.

"The Dunning-Kruger Effect?" I asked uncertainly, signaling to Lydia for another Norrlands Guld. "I'll have one, too, thanks," Johannes said and went on: "It's a cognitive bias that means someone who's incompetent is also incapable of understanding their own incompetence. An incompetent person, Dunning and Kruger suggest, overestimates their competence to a greater degree than a competent one, whereas it's not uncommon for competent people to underestimate their own competence. For example, a tradesman who's fucking shit, let's say some rubbish painter, will never accept that his work sucks, while a talented one will be more likely to underestimate his own talent: the very fact that he's talented gives him the capacity to see that he could be better. Another example: if you ask a bunch of people if they're good drivers, maybe 70 percent of them will tell you they're above average, and it goes without saying that that can't be true. So a large number of them will be overestimating their own competence.

"In your case, it seems more like you're underestimating your competence. From what little I've read, like this piece on Houellebecq, it doesn't seem inconceivable that sooner or later you'd be able to write a perfectly okay novel." Lydia put the tall tankards down on the table. "But given the strength of the doubts you seem to be having, you might ask if you even *want* to write one?"

"Yes, I probably still do. I guess."

"Hmm. But the fact that you view yourself as so fucking lazy, which in a way might actually be true, could easily become a . . . what's it called again? . . . A self-fulfilling prophecy."

He was right. Obviously I understood what I didn't understand! Or perhaps, more like: Of course I understood that I was basically *stalling*, that when it came to writing I was procrastinating, constantly trying to make excuses, including by seeing myself as completely *unimaginative*, which I'd also admitted to Johannes. Even seeing myself as lazy could in fact be one of those excuses. At the same time, I realized—not without a certain bitterness—that I would never actually be able to write anything for "the masses," and that therefore, even if I did manage to write a novel—which wasn't guaranteed by any means—it would probably only reach . . . well, maybe a few hundred readers in Sweden—and would that even be meaningful?

Before Johannes had gotten onto the so-called Dunning-Kruger Effect, which I hadn't previously heard of, I'd given him an exhaustive account of my musings around how, even in high school, I'd likely been marinated in an aesthetic that belonged to what could be described as postmodernism; an approach that in an all but fanatical sense put *text*—language and style— before content, or at least before narrative, plot.

"I suppose it was," I'd solemnly declared, "my idolization of Thomas Bernhard, that extreme textual and linguistic being, that actually made me start to hate stories—in the same way that I think Bernhard hated them."

"But why did he hate stories? . . . I mean, that sounds a bit *spazzy* for a writer."

"Yeah, that's true. Of course it's . . . yeah, a little backward, I guess."

"Very counterproductive!"

"But that's exactly why I've been questioning that approach more and more lately! Bernhard described himself as a *story destroyer*, the typical *story destroyer*. Whenever he, die-hard cynic that he was, realized he was starting to engage in storytelling— or perhaps a more conventional form of narrative—*he would shoot it down, shut it down.* That became a sort of credo for me when I got more into that kind of literature in high school; I started seeing traditional storytelling as more or less *anathema*.

"It felt," I'd gone on, "completely natural for me to identify myself exclusively with writers of so-called 'challenging' and 'high' literature; besides Thomas Bernhard, people like Peter Handke and Marguerite Duras, for example. Writers who were considered more or less *nobélisable*. It felt natural for me to picture myself not as part of the 'popular circuit,' but as part of the cultured one. But then you get older, of course, and more and more realistic, including in an economic sense, and you think," I'd argued loudly, "'Yes, perhaps I should be able to write for a wider readership after all. Without ipso facto whoring myself out completely.'"

"If you ever want to get a novel published and earn money from your writing, you should probably think on that a little more."

"Yeah, but I mean I *am* trying! Now that I've really tried to write for a wider readership, now that I've *really tried* to write broader, as it were, I'm realizing that it was probably genuinely *devastating* for me to have had, right from the start, this snobby, elitist view on writing, since that snobby and elitist view—largely influenced by Bernhard's assessment of conventional and traditional or perhaps even classical storytelling as something 'low'—or perhaps so much as 'undignified,' that is—prevented me from understanding what the most basic elements of a *straightforward story* are."

Here I had perhaps exhaled a bit before going on: "It's almost like I've consciously gone all out, in a way, to be completely useless [I might actually have used the adjective *incompetent* here]. In any case, I'd say my fixation on 'highness' has had basically devastating consequences for me."

It was in his response to this that Johannes had mentioned the so-called Dunning-Kruger Effect. Still, I wasn't prepared to wrap up my line of reasoning, my *confessional*! I wasn't quite, I thought gloomily, incompetent or genuinely comprehensively useless, since my *inadequacy* wasn't total—or at least I didn't think so—but I did have a very clear handicap; a millstone around my neck that prevented me from taking certain essential steps toward a career as a professional writer of what I felt were, you know, traditional or straightforward stories.

I ordered another beer and went on telling him about an article[*] by the conservative literary critic Carl Rudbeck that I'd googled earlier that day at Maria's kitchen table, in which the aforementioned describes how *a traditionally Aristotelian subject*, which for millennia had told stories with a *beginning, middle, and end*, had lately—indeed, in our, so to say, postmodern era (I assume Rudbeck meant)—come to be replaced by a new writing subject, *a postmodern subject* that produced only "arbitrarily ordered fragments."

"Hmm. Yeah, that does sound pretty relevant to your situation," Johannes replied with ironic zest; I realized he was already sick of my diatribes and had most likely started to view me as . . . well, unbecomingly solipsistic and conceited. When he then ordered a double shot of Jameson for himself in a way that more or less subliminally emphasized his displeasure at my self-centeredness, I felt I should probably start wrapping it up.

"Anyway," I went on with a certain stubbornness, "I don't identify as a *raconteur*, a *storyteller*. I see myself more as doomed to be a producer of the very same *disjointed fragments*

---

[*]Rudbeck, C. (February 7, 1996). "Roland Barthes *och skriet från underjorden*" ("Roland Barthes and the Cry from the Underground"), *Dagens Nyheter*.

that Rudbeck is discussing here! On the one hand, it might be due to my fixation on postmodern writers—Bernhard, for example—but on the other it could also have something to do with the fact that we live in *another era*; that we, as subjects, have actually started to see the world, indeed, everything around us, not as something with a beginning, middle, and end, but as center and periphery. Yeah, I guess that might be what Rudbeck was really saying in his article."

A meme suddenly came to mind that I'd seen on the Facebook group *Nihilist Memes*, which published nihilist memes: two figures—men, twenty-plus—in two stills from the 2006 anime version of Tatsuhiko Takimoto's manga *Welcome to the N.H.K.*

Yamazaki (in oval glasses) and the protagonist Satō (in a black polo-neck) are near (or in) something that could perhaps be a park: bare black trees, it's winter, snowflakes sail down lugubriously over the frames.

Yamazaki, his gaze turned down at the ground, says: "A drama has a progressive plot, an emotional climax, and a resolution.

"But our lives aren't like that. All we get day after day are a bunch of vague anxieties that are never really resolved."

Indeed, there's no denying that in the meme Yamazaki comes across as laconic, possibly clinically depressed, but on the other hand he's described—on English Wikipedia—as a stable person compared to Satō, who's frozen stuck in his *hikikomori* existence, his pathetic *otaku* behavior, and who—on English Wikipedia—is described as considerably more *unhinged.*

"You're not alone," Johannes said, then downed his Jameson in one. "Everyone's got postmodern brains now!" I capitulated and ordered myself a Jameson, but only a single, seeing as I had Molly to look after and all. I couldn't get too drunk while shouldering such adult responsibility. *It would,* I thought to myself, *be a veritable moral defeat to fuck up at this stage.*

"Well, it's not so surprising that you've had trouble writing mainstream stuff, I guess. You don't read all that many so-called normal novels on the whole, do you? It's not like you usually read thrillers or crime novels, is it?"

"I most definitely do not!"

"But if you *were* interested in thrillers, you'd instinctively be able to write one. If you *were* interested in conventionally told stories, then you'd be able to write more conventionally."

"That's quite possible."

"Writers who write shit-hot thrillers are probably *extremely* interested in that specific genre. They're hooked. They've read hundreds, even thousands of them. Probably going back to their early teens or something. So they're experts in . . . well, *thriller-ese,* as it were. An idiom that's obviously completely impenetrable to you—for reasons you've mentioned yourself."

"Exactly! Of course, that's it."

It cheered me that Johannes understood my hopeless position within the field of cultural production; I really wanted to belong to the *intellectual* (or perhaps *avant-garde*) end of the spectrum—but absolutely not the *commercial* one.

"I guess, on the positive side, *if you do get published*, you might have a chance to position yourself as an expert on what floats your boat, if it really is Bernhard and that kind of literature. For example, someone like John Ajvide Lindqvist probably wouldn't have been able to write as good a horror novel as *Let the Right One In* had he not known his chops when it came to horror. He's fucking talented, mind, maybe even verging on genius."

Johannes definitely had a point there. Obviously Ajvide Lindqvist wasn't just some opportunist who'd suddenly upped and decided to write a personal, occasionally gross but above all deeply moving book about vampires! He'd plausibly read up *a lot* about vampires—no? Wasn't it likely that he was basically *pathologically* into horror as a genre? Anything else was, I thought—or perhaps even *felt*—completely implausible.

"The ability," I started solemnly, "to produce, as a writer, a text that meets the quality criteria of a specific genre should call for a genuine—well, 'authentic' interest in the genre from the writer's side."

Should one get it into their head to transpose the Ajvide Lindqvist example to my own situation, *which it only later occurred to me to do*, one might well be able to say the same thing about me, no? The genre that I had long since had a soft spot for as a reader, and with which I was well acquainted, having consumed it for over a decade, was obviously also the genre that I myself wrote in, or at was least *trying* to write in: *transgressive postmodern prose*, one might say, represented internationally by writers such as William S. Burroughs, J. G. Ballard, Kathy Acker, Dennis Cooper, Charles Bukowski, Anthony Burgess, Bret Easton Ellis, Chuck Palahniuk, Michel Houellebecq, et cetera, et cetera.

Now, it has to be said, several of these writers did sell some of their titles in the hundreds of thousands of copies, but it would nevertheless be a shame to say that they belonged to the *popular circuit* or the field of literary production's commercial pole. Perhaps they were simply situated in the borderlands between the popular and learned—and perhaps that was precisely why I found them so appealing?

My intense self-pity at being unable to tell a straightforward story, it occurs to me now in hindsight, may well have seemed downright psychopathological, but Johannes, who by then had endured my narcissistic babbling for a while, had humored me all the same. In any case, he suddenly gave me a both tender and self-righteous look.

"I really hope you aren't planning on writing about the struggle of being a writer," he said.

"No, definitely not. What made you think that?"

"If you make the blunder of writing about 'writer's block,' then be prepared for a critical *mauling*. Since what it's essentially saying is that you have nothing to say—which maybe you don't, for that matter."

"That's possible. Now that you mention it."

"Personally, I think—in my more grandiose moments—that *I* have things to say. In real life, as it were. But obviously I don't write novels. But just so you know: as an urban, middle-class man approaching middle age, to write about something as fucking sappy as writer's block is basically to commit literary suicide."

Obviously I agreed with that. That all the more men had in recent years stooped to writing about the struggle of living their privileged, white, not infrequently *heterosexual* and masculine middle-class lives as writerly (or perhaps *writerly blocking*) personas was perhaps a trend of the day—and it was true that these "cis men" were sitting ducks for cruel, gender-enlightened, identity-politics pens in the press. But at the end of the day, what was one actually supposed to write about if one had a postmodern brain and was self-aware to the point of insanity? Especially if, as Carl Rudbeck believed, it was indeed true that the influence of postmodernism had created a postmodern subject with no beginning or end, but instead a center and periphery?

"One reason why aspiring writers can't, don't want to, or don't dare tell so-called straightforward stories could actually be down to a fear of exposing themselves," Johannes philosophized. "I mean, maybe they're afraid, afraid of exposing—of *compromising* themselves. In trying to emulate a traditional Aristotelian subject, they would give away the fact that they simply aren't capable of functioning like one. Perhaps it's not even a matter of incompetence, but of *impotence*. Writers can't order the world they live in anymore. They're out of touch with reality."

Indeed, what could anyone write about, if not one's own impotence in a world without hierarchies? Telling a straightforward story wasn't just difficult, it was as good as a "crime" in a reality as complex as ours. Johannes was right. Rudbeck was right. It wasn't at all unreasonable—not at all—that a crevice had opened up, a gaping chasm, in fact, between the older (dead) and younger human narrators in postmodernity's liberal (and, so much the worse, fragmenting) democracies. And yet the popular writers, the Aristotelian-*lites*, as it were, and possibly yuppie pigs, went on telling their meaningless stories with beginnings, middles, and ends, as has been their custom for centuries. But these stories had all been told before. They were just repetitions. The same old tangy regurgitations. Conversely, the stories that *weren't* being told—or the artistic works that were as yet unwritten—could be produced only by post-Aristotelian, fragmented subjects (reared in an existence of maximal entropy), and these were, frankly, I thought much later, not yet ripe for this desolate practice; besides, we didn't even know whether these writers had been born yet.

In the "Houellebecq Text" I had, if nothing else, I thought, succeeded in keeping within the *unities of action, place, and time—*

here I started gesticulating pretty wildly—and in that respect I had succeeded in writing a straightforward story, or at the very least a functioning scene; something intelligible—cogent, as it were; something that followed the model of classical drama. The "Houellebecq Text" may have seemed riven from a greater context, sure, but I felt I had nevertheless succeeded in giving the impression that what was being recounted was very much being recounted by a so-called traditional Aristotelian subject. Still, I was feeling highly uncertain, uncomfortable, and all too self-aware, and was, as previously mentioned, quite nervous ahead of Johannes's critique (which I knew could be harsh but fair).

Johannes flicked slightly stiffly through his printout and said that the "Houellebecq Text" may have had a certain "credibility issue," but he stressed that he'd found it hard to avoid doing a chiefly psychologizing reading of the text, *seeing as obviously he knew me personally*, as he put it, *as a close friend, even*, and he couldn't get away from that, as it were.

Initially he'd been struck by the fact that I'd clearly felt a strong need to emulate Houellebecq—"You're impersonating Houellebecq! Mimicking his 'software.'"—but that had also perhaps been the rub, he admitted, even though, as he said, he thought the text worked well. It was even pretty "entertaining," he stated drily, that is, without looking like he really meant it.

"But what's the appeal of Houellebecq to you? Why does someone like you feel the need to impersonate him?—Yeah, a pretty interesting question, huh?"

"Sure, yeah, I think so," I was forced to concede, "but isn't that kind of why people write in the first place? If I'd known exactly what I was doing I'd—"

"I mean it's easy to see why someone as fucking bullheaded as Houellebecq," Johannes interrupted, "would appeal to people way more *inhibited* than him."

"Well, obviously I'm more inhibited than Houellebecq!" I said, gesturing for another two beers, and a double of Jameson.

"I'm sure many are."

"There's something in that, of course. He's . . . extremely *unconstrained*," I said thoughtfully, "but at the same time there's a thinking behind that *unconstrainedness*. There's a *method*—a *methodology*—to his . . . to his *filterlessness*. Yeah, I don't know how to explain it."

"He's capable of something that you aren't?"

"Well, I mean obviously he's a *genius*, more or less. Obviously I couldn't write a novel like *The Elementary Particles*. But on the other hand he's the only one who *could* have written *The Elementary Particles*."

"Still, the question remains! Who *is* this person who feels the need to impersonate Houellebecq? . . ."

Well, obviously I had no answer to that.

If I was indeed impersonating Houellebecq, it was perhaps to understand something of his brutality, I thought, to understand the writer's masochistic brutality toward himself, and his more or less sadistic brutality toward his own characters. Yes, there must have been a reason why I fantasized about this

French writer so much as to impersonate him (i.e., beyond my pretext of it being an *homage*).

Johannes started to mumble that it was perhaps a form of aggression on my part, but quickly waved it off and instead claimed I'd clearly been *going flat out* when Houellebecq was spewing bile about that girl with anorexia at Monoprix, but that I had *hit the brakes* or gotten almost "oddly restrained" when he got onto Batman and Robin. Obviously he didn't want to hurt me, he assured me, but he still had to tell it like it was, since he couldn't help but reflect on it all.

"When Houellebecq spews bile about that anorexic, it's kind of like the mimicry works. It becomes correct. Your own affected feelings about a fictional girl with anorexia and Houellebecq's feelings do feel pretty believable, entirely *commensurate*. But when it comes to Batman and Robin, a clearly homoerotic *trope*, this incongruence starts to come out, since *I*—your friend—can see that you, the one impersonating Houellebecq, would have loved to write a lot more decadently about those pretty fruity characters."

"What's that supposed to mean?"

"Well, I may be wrong, but I do think you'd have liked to write something way more twisted and *pervy* about Batman and Robin. But even *you*—when you're writing all that—can tell that the real Houellebecq wouldn't be interested in all that stuff in the same way. And then it's like you're holding back . . . like you're withholding something depraved that the Houellebecq character might have actually said in that text. The only problem is that that would be out of character. Surely you must have noticed that yourself at some point, I mean, when you were writing it—that Batman and Robin just don't 'tickle' Houellebecq all that much? That's more . . . well, more your shtick."*

"There may be something in that."

"But, well, you know, if the reader doesn't know you then I don't really think they'll give it a second thought. But if they do know you then . . . well, then they'll see—I reckon—I imagine—that you're really just wanting to put the pedal to the metal and write something more or less vile that Houellebecq might actually say about Batman and Robin, but that you're holding back, that you're . . . well, *definitely* hitting the brakes. That you're actually shutting it down in almost the same way that you say Bernhard would shut down any impulse toward conventional storytelling."

For a brief moment I wanted to brush off Johannes's shameless analysis by declaring that we were way too drunk for a level-

---

*I knew full well what Johannes was alluding to by this "your shtick." Of course, he couldn't have failed to see the Instagram posts from the autumn 2017 costume party thrown by Maria's extremely homophile, aristocratic, and not exactly hard-up cousin Ludvig (variously known as "Luds," "Ludders," or "Luddsy" by his devoutly upper-class guests) and his boyfriend, Alexander, at their detached pad in Skår. Alexander was dressed as King Gustav III and seized every chance he got that night to pinch Maria's cheek in a way that eventually felt more icky than charming.—And yes, we had in fact gone dressed as Batman and Robin. However, it had *not* been my idea; as I recall I'd been highly skeptical at first, but had eventually given my consent. Thanks to Maria's theater contacts we were also able to satisfy the hosts' exacting aesthetic requirements on costume quality. Ludvig would no doubt have held us in contempt had we deigned to show up in sheets (as ghosts) or wrapped in toilet paper (mummies).

headed discussion about the "Houellebecq Text" (which now felt thoroughly besmirched by Johannes's analytical perspicacity), but since I realized that wasn't actually true (us being too drunk, that is), I let it go. There was no denying that Johannes had put his finger on something. There was, I was forced to admit, a truth to his observation. Since, on the one hand, I definitely had been going flat out when I'd had Houellebecq spew bile about the girl with anorexia at Monoprix, but on the other hand, I realized, I'd pretty much done an emergency stop once he'd gotten onto the "Dynamic Duo."

"But I do actually write that Houellebecq himself says he's not so interested in that 'flying rat and his little friend,'" I wheedily put forward.

"But that's because *you realize it's true!*" Johannes said triumphantly. "Really, it would be more realistic," he went on, "depending on what you're going for, that is, if that pig's surname wasn't Grayson and they essentially just *never mentioned* Batman and Robin."

Indeed, that the French writer would even care about something like that cop having the same name as Bruce Wayne/ Batman's teenage adept and would additionally mention Wertham's *The Seduction of the Innocent* because a friend had gone on a rant about it on a bender the night before—yes, perhaps that was a tad unrealistic? Indeed, it was. I could see that myself (even if I was offended by this kind of boundless criticism). And thus what I had written had gone against its purpose, especially if realism was indeed what I'd been looking to achieve. Which I suppose it was? It was also hardly believable that the real Houellebecq, like myself, would have read Will Brooker's thesis *Batman Unmasked*, which explored these aspects of the masked hero in depth.

Nor could I conjure up the illusion that even a fictive Houellebecq would ever have gone onto French Amazon and ordered a used copy of that same title for €43.79, or even the Kindle format for €13.03. (Obviously he didn't even own a Kindle!) Houellebecq was no such geek, and *queer* geek he most certainly was not, not in any shape or form.

8

ARE YOU AN NPC?

It had taken me an alarmingly long time to realize where I was when I woke up the next morning from a pretty nasty dream. For a while I'd even thought I was tied up in some way, since my arms were locked in an odd position; during that tropical night I'd also tangled myself up in a sheet that was troublingly wet. Once I'd managed to unbind myself I realized, in any case, that I was in Maria's bedroom. I exhaled. I was on terra firma. Only too soon, however, a ream of anxiety-laden questions lined up one after the other.

Had I pissed myself in Maria's bed? How had I gotten home? Had I well and truly disgraced myself the previous night? . . . The first question seemed relatively easy to answer, at least: I smelled the sheet. It didn't smell, at least not of piss, so I therefore drew the optimistic conclusion that it was just cold sweats.

Anyway, the lion's share of my brain had been focused on processing my unpleasant dream. In it, I had been standing with Molly in my arms in another one of those terrifyingly insanity-spattered—*destroyed* and *demolished*—rooms, where it was as though a reckless blast of disinhibition had blown all the furnishings away. There were no windows. Conversely, there was something that could well have represented a door, but which in fact consisted solely of a big dented and water-logged sheet of corrugated cardboard covering an uneven rectangular opening in the wall that had been gnawed out by creepy-crawlies; a "door" no more practical than a retarded kid's *drawing* of a door on a piece of paper. I had, I clearly remembered, stood paralyzed before this joke of a door, this archetypal *nondoor*, just waiting for the unwholesome creatures that had gathered outside to throw aside their inhibitions, force the door, come inside, and violate both Molly and myself. Indeed, what were they waiting for? What was holding them back? Perhaps a mere magic seal, an esoteric hobo sign, was all that prevented them from tearing us to shreds?—Another question struck me with an intensity as sudden as it was extreme:

Where is Molly?

As I asked myself this question I felt a strong groundswell of nausea inside me. Luckily I made it to the bathroom in time, and I spent a good while on my knees praying to the porcelain god, as they say. After that I cupped my shaking hands under the tap and managed to drink a few gulps of water that I immediately puked up again. Only after I'd dragged myself back to bed did I remember the question that had been sidelined during my bout of acute nausea. *Where the fuck is Molly?* If Molly was dead or somehow incapacitated or stolen or a runaway, I would never be able to forgive myself! I started calling her name—to no avail. I cried out even louder—but heard no barks, no scratch of little claws on parquet. I got anxious. If something serious had happened to Molly, I would take my own life, I thought, since at least then I wouldn't ever have to face Maria. There was literally no other alternative. If Molly was dead—then, yes, I was too.

To some extent *boosted* by these bleak future prospects, and with a burst of energy that surprised even myself (given how hungover I was), I started rushing here and there in Maria's apartment, from room to room, calling the little dog's name. She wasn't in the kitchen, or the living room, or the hall, or the bedroom, toilet, or stairwell. Or the closets or the lower kitchen cabinets. My eyes welled up all the more as I heard the panic rising in my scarily cracked and jittery voice. She was nowhere to be found!

I tried to get hold of Johannes to ask what had actually happened the night before. Perhaps he had forcibly removed Molly from my care? *That wasn't actually such a long shot,* I told myself and felt my pulse slowly start to lower a little. *Surely he must*

*have seen how drunk I was? He could just as well have decided I
didn't deserve to keep custody of the dog.* When Johannes didn't
pick up I started texting him: "What happened yesterday? Have
you seen Molly?"

Yes, if it was true that I'd somehow lost Molly . . . my life
would undoubtedly be over. I went into the bathroom. Vom-
med again. Flushed, then sat down on the seat. Scratched my
face a little. The world—time and space—was still spinning
disquietingly around me. *I should die right here on the spot*, I
thought—I wanted to puke myself out of the world!—but, just
as I was preparing to take a deep breath and scream out in lim-
bic anxiety and raw despair like a savage and obscene jungle
beast, I heard a quiet whimper from somewhere. Molly! Yes,
surely what I had just heard could only be the whimper of a diminutive dog?! But from where? Where? I hardly dared breathe.
But then I heard it again! Without daring to hope too much, I
cautiously whispered the little pooch's name. Yes, *there, there*,
she has to be *there*, down in the laundry basket itself! And so it
was. Thank goodness!

I lifted the white plastic lid and saw a blue-and-yellow IKEA
bag—which was moving. In the bag lay a towel (Ralph Lau-
ren) and, wrapped up in it, Molly the dog, on a pile of Maria's
and my underwear, T-shirts, et cetera. I carefully lifted her up
and gave her a quick examination—she seemed bewildered,
but generally . . . yeah, pretty okay (actually)—and then I cried
(literal) tears of gratitude for a while. But perhaps the tears
contained more than that; it had been completely *awful*—

monstrous—of me to subject a fragile little dog to that kind of treatment. Molly was no doubt shattered, but surprisingly enough she didn't seem to hold any major grudge against me. When she would patently be within her rights to take a leap straight at my carotid, no?

Though, of course, this type of dog is, understandably enough, very timid. Physically she seemed totally okay, but her fur was a little wet and tousled. Might that be why I'd put her in the laundry basket in the first place? Because I, in my in-toxication, had taken her for an object in need of laundering? Perhaps.

When I sniffed her I noticed that she did smell of alcohol, or beer, to be precise. As such, it was likely that I (*or perhaps someone else*) had spilled a beer over her. Yes, that was prob-ably how it had gone down, I thought in shame, since Molly blatantly smelled like she had literally been bathed in beer.

This was exactly what Johannes confirmed when I man-aged to get hold of him a little later. I (*and no one else*) had at some point—either by mistake or perhaps even deliberately (Johannes had been in the toilet when it happened)—tipped a beer over Molly at Bar Kino's outdoor terrace next to Hagabion cinema. Having helped me to wipe Molly down with a wad of napkins, he had simply and sharply ordered me to go home. An order that I—thankfully—had followed. Unfortunately I had no memory of this whatsoever. Fact is, I couldn't even remember having been at Kino.

Once I could breathe a little more easy, after rinsing off the poor, beer-soused thing and shampooing her with Espree Silky Show (a premium shampoo that promotes a healthy, glossy coat in toy dog breeds), I did in fact start to recall us getting a drink at Haket's outdoor terrace (where we'd probably made a pit stop before we, or, rather, Johannes, called time on the rager at Kino, which was also very close to Maria's place). I remembered that I'd talked *a lot* about playing golf in Ibiza and had then been struck by the irrefutable and additionally very pleasurable conviction that I was in fact on that Mediterranean island right then; or I was, I had felt, in both Gothenburg and Ibiza *simultaneously*.

Much more clearly I remembered how, after leaving Plankan in high spirits, we'd sat down at Oceanen in Stigbergstorget, where Johannes—who, truth be told, at that point had seemed more drunk than me—had started saying increasingly politically incorrect things, especially about women.

Now, I might admittedly have been the one to set off the windbag in him, because I'd initially told him I was thinking of renovating my bathroom, only to—after a bit of coaxing on his part—admit it was in fact because Maria had expressed a certain horror at its state.

"Women love clean bathrooms because they're filthy pigs," he said.

I laughed in pure shock.

"It's why they're obsessed with *ablutions*, too," he went on.

"It's piss-easy to turn women on by telling them they're filthy, that they've got bad genes, et cetera."

Brushing aside these unpleasant bizarreries, I'd started telling him that, ever since seeing *Blade Runner 2049*, my thoughts about Maria had actually been taking ever weirder trajectories. Trajectories that both amused and concerned me. Would it actually matter to me, I'd told Johannes that I'd asked myself, if Maria was a hologram just like the replicant's (a.k.a. Ryan Gosling's) hologram girlfriend in Denis Villeneuve's film? Would it actually be any issue if she was an *android*? An entirely artificial person? Might that thought, I'd asked Johannes, perhaps have something to do with "derealization"? Was that why for some time (the last few weeks) I'd successively started viewing Maria as an increasingly . . . well, *unreal* being? Johannes had remarked laconically that Western culture bred both derealization and depersonalization.

"Perhaps it's not so much that I view Maria as *robotic*," I'd assured him, "but . . . well, she *is* more robotic than I am . . . in her ability to be . . . uh, *completely representative*. Out of the blue she might start talking with this completely authoritative and exaggeratedly grown-up voice; a voice entirely different to the one she usually has, and I *know*—I *know*—that voice is totally put-on."

"It's not authentic?"

"You know, I don't know. She's so . . . well, *formal*, in short. Very formal."

"*She*'s not authentic?"

"Yeah, maybe not, because I can see it's just for show. A bit like when you exaggerate your accent to blend in around people who are . . . well, menials or something . . . Anyway, I think Maria's much more of a *normie* than me."

"Well, she's not exactly a philosopher! But in her defense, you could also argue that there are no female philosophers per se."

"But surely there have to be some?"

"Who then? Name one!"

I desperately racked my brain for a name.

"Given that you had to think for a fucking age just to come up with one, you should still be able to admit that there are basically none," Johannes said after I'd managed to squeeze out one name:

Simone de Beauvoir.

Johannes declared that de Beauvoir was trash and added that women, in a way, weren't even people, not deep down. I'd sighed, but my ears had started to prick up all the same.

"In any case they're not *fully fledged* people. Their inner worlds are generally completely uninteresting. They lack agency and critical thinking. They hate people who don't follow conventions. They react extremely negatively to lines of thought that aren't politically correct. Peterson's right. People who break with prevalent norms are snakes in women's eyes. Or at the very least some kind of substitute for a mythological beast who threatens their offspring. And their offspring is basically the only thing they're programmed to care about in the slightest. (Best case.) They're NPCs."*, **

I must admit that I laughed at Johannes's nasty view of women—which I certainly didn't share, *nota bene*, not in any shape or form!—but at the same time I couldn't help but be hypnotized by his bizarreries; in moments like these my friend could be pretty entertaining, if not spellbinding.

I assume that it was also somewhere around here that I pulled out my notebook (Moleskine) and started scribbling down as much as I could of what he was saying. (Something that would prove enormously helpful to me in my reconstruction of these rather fuzzy memories.)

I have no memory of trying to defend Woman from Johannes's cynical attack, which would probably have been pointless anyway, but I do seem to remember making a point of assuring him that I definitely didn't consider Maria "soul-

---

*NPC, *non-player character* or *non-playable character*, is a term from the gaming/role-playing world that denotes a character who is controlled by the computer in a video or role-playing game. An NPC is often characterized by having prewritten replies. Since 2016 the term has also been used as a metaphor for a certain type of person (on platforms such as 4chan, et cetera): "[NPCs are] the kind of people who make a show of discomfort when you break the status quo like by breaking the normie barrier to invoke a real discussion." (Anonymous, "Are You an NPC?," *4chan* [July 7, 2016]).
**"90 percent of any population are going to be NPCs, and 10 percent are going to be the innovators. [. . .] The vast majority of humans are non-player characters. They have no mind outside their programming." (Rogan, J. [Host]. [November 8, 2018]. Michael Malice [#1197]. *The Joe Rogan Experience*).

less" in any way. Absolutely not! The question that *Blade Runner 2049* had sparked in me was more about whether it was irrelevant to the love I felt for Maria if she was a robot or not.

"My love," I solemnly attested, "wouldn't be essentially different even if she was a robot. It wouldn't matter, plain and simple! So long as she had the same *software*, that is."

If on top of that she could rouse my desires, I reasoned further, did it really make any difference what she was made of?

"Though, of course, I probably couldn't bring myself to love her if she was just a sexless hologram, a complete chimera. If I wasn't a sexless hologram myself, that is."

"Maybe that's kinda what the film's about, too," Johannes said in a melancholy tone of voice.

"What do you mean?"

"If some of us were artificial it wouldn't matter, so long as the feelings we have—and are capable of expressing—are so authentic that we can't even tell the difference between artificial and, so to say, real-person feelings. If we generally couldn't tell robots from humans, then . . . well, we'd be ethically obliged to treat robots like people. Even if Maria, like most women, is potentially an NPC, that doesn't give you the right to spit in her face. Even if ninety percent of the world's population were NPCs, it wouldn't give the other ten the right to enslave the majority."

"No, of course. That would be daft."

"It makes no difference if you're an artificial person or just a fictional character—humanity still has *a biological imperative*

for empathy that trumps all technology . . . indeed, an imperative greater than any *mind games*."

Our conversation was interrupted by a call from Maria.
After a moment's hesitation, I decided not to pick up. Because
then she would have heard all the hullabaloo on Oceanen's terrace. She would have heard I was drunk. And since I'd had to
look after Molly for over two weeks—*You're taking good care
of Molly, right?*—*Sure I am!*—I really didn't want her to get the
impression I was out *on the skids*, which would obviously be
the only impression she would get if I did answer.

Fuck, I thought when Johannes got up to go take a leak and
get another round, *why did he have to insist Maria was an NPC?*
Surely she couldn't be? I mean, it was for her, for Maria, that
young lady with the diminutive breasts, that I had become—
indeed, *forced* myself to become—an increasingly normative
human, a person who had largely submitted to unspoken yet
undeniable requirements that I be more of a "normie" as it
were, since with Maria the thought of chilling and cooking and
taking long walks and enduring soulless romantic comedies at
the cinema and arranging double dates and watching Netflix
actually didn't sicken me—quite the reverse!

The thought of being *authentically* tender toward Maria,
as if she were a part of myself, a *kindred spirit* pretty much,
had not for one second sparked my instinctive, immediate, and
fanatical contempt of the *middle-class consciousness*, or the offensive and hetero-hegemonic *dime-a-dozen state* with which

I associated all these more or less parodically relationship-related thoughts, feelings, and behaviors. It was Maria and no one else who had caused me to mature—indeed, to grow as a person, as it were, and to a far greater extent than I had ever thought possible!

In this way I still regarded my relationship with Maria as something *fantastic* in spite of it all, I told myself as I sat there, and as something that I—de facto no exaggeration—supposed I could thank God that I had gotten to experience. But I also realized, as I swiped aside Maria's incoming call on my smartphone, that I was nevertheless capable of admitting, on an intuitive plane at least, that Johannes could possibly be right. That Maria truly was an NPC wasn't at all out of the question; the thought had actually crossed my mind, too.

After Johannes had gotten back to the table with two beers, we got onto Houellebecq again.

Johannes went on delivering highly interesting opinions. Especially when it came to my own fixation on the French writer.

"You're just not rooted in *reality*," he said in the end. "Houellebecq has paid for his successes by losing his teeth! Could you stomach paying that price? That you can so much as imagine Maria being a hologram shows that she doesn't live in the real world, either. The both of you have it way too good. You're so healthy you . . . well, you hardly have any bodies. You have no body. Maria has no body. So, holograms. But a person needs a . . . well, a sickly body . . . a sickly flesh, in order to access real philosophical reflections.

"A person can't be real if they have no contact with suffering, and they can't have contact with suffering if they don't have a body. People who don't suffer, who don't have cancer, are simply not real.

"Houellebecq presumably didn't need to lose his teeth, but for some reason—one might even be able to call it a truly *spiritual* reason—he chose to lose them anyway. Since that was the price to be paid. Naturally that's why he's so interesting to you, because you're not *there* and you can't *be there*, either. Because for you there is no suffering. Because you haven't chosen it yet. You can't choose it.

"In your defense, one could argue that you've to some degree intuitively understood his genius. You need Houellebecq as a *mask*. You have a psychological need for that mask, and it doesn't even matter if what you do with it becomes a parody or a failure. For most *normies*, Houellebecq's just a cynical, pessimistic clown. They refuse to see that *The Elementary Particles* is about the West's downfall. In Houellebecq they see only an amusing contraindicator that they use to calibrate their own values so that they follow as representative a paradigm as possible. They have no real contact with his material. They don't want it. The more experienced among them obviously realize that they've been well and truly buggered by globalization the whole time. But they are few. On the other hand, perhaps way too many of our own generation still can't wrap their heads around the fact that they'll never earn as much as our Greta Thunberg–loving boomer parents.

"The main question here is whether Houellebecq actually does any good through his work if ninety percent of his readers still don't even twig postmodernity's murder-fuck of society. For fuck's sake, what he's describing is Ragnarök! But the Gen X reader and the MTV generation will never bring themselves to *own* Ragnarök! Never! And in the grand scheme of things it doesn't actually matter; they read Houellebecq with a glint in their eyes because they've heard he's one of Europe's greatest writers. That he achieved that position by losing his teeth or making a sacrifice that those NPC peeps couldn't even contemplate making isn't even a blip on the radar. Because no one wants to be a suffering body; no one wants to live in the real world.

"No one *actually* wants to be exposed to any philosophical reflection whatsoever. No one wants to be confronted with *existence*."

By the time I'd rinsed off and then walked Molly in the shade of the old turn-of-the-century houses that lined Linnégatan (it was a shorter walk than usual) it was already eleven a.m. Back at home, I plied her with water and food, and Johannes—after copious unanswered calls and texts—was finally so kind as to call me back and I could thus fill the gaps in my memory from the night before. For what it's worth, Johannes also claimed to be hungover. With a laugh, he described how ashamed I'd been at having "bathed" Molly in beer at Kino, though he also admitted that he certainly hadn't ruled out the possibility that I'd tipped the beer onto her on purpose, since I'd been giving her the "evil eye" for a good while before the incident. What could have prompted such wrath, however, he didn't dare guess. I assured him that it was implausible—actually basically impossible—that I would ever intentionally bathe that little dog in beer.[*]

After the call I fell asleep fully clothed and was woken up a few hours later by Molly lying on my chest, staring me dead in the eyes like a little sphinx (or Incubus). It was actually kind of scary.

Anyway, I felt how I deserved to feel. In a few short hours Maria would be home and in all probability moody that I hadn't returned her call or messages. She would also take me to task, no doubt, for neglecting to post any nice shots on Molly's god-damn Instagram account. Still, what tormented me most was my guilt at having almost killed the little minx.

Had Molly been forced to spend just a few more hours in that laundry basket—in the hottest, lightest hours of the day, say, that is, between ten and two (or thereabouts)—she would have

---

[*]By the way, I never did tell him I'd found Molly in the laundry basket in the end. Instead I cobbled together a story about finding her under the sofa, where she'd suffered a possible heatstroke, which was why—indeed, in her semiconscious state—she hadn't replied to my calls. You could almost say I'd saved her life. Yup, when all was said and done I was practically a *hero*, I'd said.

breathed her last, guaranteed. The laundry basket stood at the foot end of the bathtub, a part of the bathroom that was at that particular time of day—especially in those weeks when the sky was an eternally bright blue—positively teeming with ultraviolet radiation, like a great big bouncing sunbeam made of porcelain, tile, and mirror. It was sheer luck I'd found her in time!

Tormented by the realization of just how close this particular shave had been, I decided to try to "ground" myself in some way, as it were. A hair of the dog consisting of a beer and perhaps a Jäger, too—Johannes's immediate suggestion on hearing how wrecked I sounded—thus felt like a good idea (that or a fantastically good bad idea), and since no other ideas were forthcoming, I clipped on Molly's lead and set out for Linnéterrassen bar, which was just a stone's throw away.

Even after my first sip of beer I could tell it was probably the height of fecklessness to extend or resume my bender just hours before Maria's return, but taking the edge off my anxiety was a top priority, to put it mildly, plus there was a chance that Maria's train would be delayed due to the tracks buckling in the heat, or at least I had my fingers firmly crossed for as much. What I was doing, I told myself, was completely reasonable under the circumstances; the beer was hitting the spot, the Jäger, too. I smiled self-consciously at the pleasant staff. Of course they should have guessed that I was more or less wrecked, but apparently I was deemed upstanding enough to be served.

Molly looked like she was feeling grand in the warm breeze

out on the terrace. Perhaps she was only mildly pooped after her night in the laundry basket. The shower, comb-out, food, and water appeared to have done her good. As I gave Molly the visual once-over I suddenly got the feeling that I was radiating with all my being an intense love for the little creature; that this love was a great force that I wrapped around her, as it were. We connected in some way. But soon the sadness came over me.

Had I not let alcohol occupy all too great a place in my life? Didn't I risk developing a veritable dependence on this insidious drug? Surely I wasn't the only one to have heard variants of: "Had alcohol been discovered today, it would have been outlawed immediately!" It was a trite thing to say, of course, but still. And people inevitably tended to validate such a statement by agreeing with it, *even if they didn't really agree with it at all*. Surely it should be impossible, I argued, to imagine alcohol of all things never existing at some point in human history? Had we not been drinking wine for millennia? What did the ancient Egyptian pharaohs drink? What was Homer's tipple? Or Socrates's? A culture, a single civilization without alcohol as an intoxicant?

Unthinkable.

The majority of us mere mortals probably wouldn't even have been fucked forth were it not for alcohol's inhibition-suppressant effect. Food for thought. *Come to think of it, what would Peterson think of this episode in my life?* Not that he was my sensei in any way. No, definitely not! Still, I did think that, had he been my analyst, he would have viewed the write-up of my past twenty-four hours with thinly veiled contempt—no, wait, the opposite, a *thickly veiled* contempt. He would be the consummate professional, might even spin some yarns about his own hangover days. (He'd definitely had his fair share of those; he said so in *12 Rules*.) But behind this formally empathic facade he would basically view me as a *chaos person*. Would he even go so far as to be ashamed of his analysand? In the same way that I myself was ashamed of my own existence? Peterson would never get that drunk. Peterson would *never* risk becoming dependent on anything at all! He was the antithesis of dependency! I thought.[*] No, I probably wouldn't find any deeper understanding from that clean-living man.

Compared to . . . well, Houellebecq, say, I'm really just an amateur at boozing, no? I would never be capable of going flat out in the same way as that giant; after all, I still had a long way to go before I risked losing my teeth! Indeed, by and large, I reasoned, the whole thing wasn't such a disaster. Actually. Molly was alive, thankfully. I was alive. We were both okay. The alcohol was unquestionably starting to make me feel a little better—or even pretty damn good.

I started flicking through the notes in my notebook from the previous night. To begin with they were relatively well

---

[*]At this point in time, I and millions of others were highly ignorant of Peterson's severe benzodiazepine (Clonazepam) dependency. His efforts to quit the class-C drug eventually led him to Russia for treatment in January 2020. There he was put in an induced coma for eight days. He was then out of the limelight for over a year.

written, but the later ones were more or less illegible. Anyway, it looked like I'd written "NPC Boomer" and "Greta Thunberg" and "Sámi Real Doll" on one of the pages. I could only guess what that was all about. Besides, by now I was starting to feel in audaciously good spirits. *Undeservedly* audaciously good spirits? Yes, perhaps. But why should they be *undeserved*, really? Everything was fine! Kind of. I hadn't sozzled away anything valuable. My hands were clean, as they say. Or at least not completely wrecked, not fucked-up beyond repair; the beer had helped, the Jäger had helped. Okay, so maybe I wasn't all that *clean* in a spiritual sense, so to speak, like an angel or a saint, but at least I didn't feel so inwardly defiled that I was willing to die in the foreseeable future.

Fact was, it had been nice to have a little cry. I'd hugged Molly and carried her like "the last drop of water" (as the writer Björn Ranelid exhorts us to carry our children), and it had been genuinely pleasant to feel such an intense gratitude that she was alive, so, more or less *inspired* by this *numinous* gratitude, I had fixed her up with Espree Silky Show and dried her white coat with Maria's posh Remington hairdryer, then painstakingly combed it out—and that was why she was looking *tip-top* again! That is, no harm done.

Having spent a while conferring with myself as to whether it would be a good bad idea to get another beer, I decided to push the boat out and ordered another beer *and* a Jäger, and then started pondering whether what Johannes had said the previous night had potentially hurt me somehow. I took all that stuff about women being filthy pigs deep down with a very large pinch of salt. That Maria—like so many others—was possibly an NPC, however, was not something I was prepared to rule out completely. But that she was supposedly a "filthy pig" just because she liked clean bathrooms was a totally hysterical proposition.

I, too, liked clean bathrooms, I reasoned, though I genuinely didn't have the capacity to keep my own bathroom clean and tidy. Between my filthy bathroom and my self—such as I perceived my filthy inner world—there was *a congruence that worked*, I thought. Had my bathroom been as nice as a woman's, I'd probably have interpreted it as a sign that I'd been feminized in some way. But if, contrary to expectation, my bathroom was as spotless as Maria's—well, in that case I'd probably be fully homosexual, I guessed.

What was it that Peterson said? You enter a person's home and realize that the person is a so-called hoarder (i.e., neurologically disturbed): all around you see hundreds of boxes, filled with masses of shit. The place is completely cluttered with thousands of bits and bobs that eat up most of its surfaces, as the hoarder saves anything they can, no exceptions: screw caps, the tops of toothpaste tubes—indeed, all sorts of tubes: tomato paste, fish roe, mayo—old newspapers, advertising brochures, bills, flyers, razors, soaps, dead wasps, et cetera, et cetera. Nothing can be chucked. Everything has a value—

or, rather, *nothing can be parted with.* So anyway: chaos. Not order. Chaos. One might think: *Is this the person's home, or is this her* existence? To which Peterson would remark that there is no difference. The analogy is total. That is, it's *both* the person's home and her existence. At the highest level of what is known as psychological integration, there is simply no difference between this person and how she organizes the objective world.

Perhaps it was time to redo my bathroom after all, I reasoned. But I also realized that I would be able to embark upon such a project only once my glistening vision of this newly renovated bathroom—as yet unexposed to decades of wear—corresponded to my inner conception of myself as someone who seriously deserved such a room. With the memory of having almost killed Molly—that innocent little lass—still fresh on my mind, not to mention all my other signs of immaturity—I realized I wasn't quite *there.*

By the time Maria finally got home I had a total of two beers and two Jägers under my belt, that's to say on top of the alcohol already in my bloodstream from the previous day's imbibements, and I was—I should probably admit—not exactly the better for wear. In spite of this, I managed to appear extremely happy to see her again (which I was, actually). Molly had completely lost her mind when she'd heard the keys in the front door and had shot off into the hallway. Maria had cuddled with her for a while and then turned her attention to me. Clearly she could see I wasn't quite fresh as a daisy, but still I felt the need to lie about the night before. Yup, there had definitely been too many beers, no doubt, but it had been a short one. We'd gotten home by nine and watched some Netflix. What had I watched? Uh, I couldn't quite remember, actually, I'd probably flicked between a bunch of things before dozing off on the couch.

Once the interrogation was over, Maria went straight on to tell me about one of her fellow passengers on the train and their extremely rowdy kids. Almost parodically *working class*, she said of the family, and she swore to never ever travel second class again. In her defense, I should say she made this remark without any real animosity in her posh voice. She was very happy to be home. Fact is, she positively radiated vitality. If she really was a hologram, she was a sharp, luminous one, pulsating with spunk. For a second I actually thought that she looked like she'd just gotten laid.

Maria shoved her wheeled Samsonite into the bedroom and started unpacking what she'd bought in the capital: clothes of various types, Dana Thomas's *Gods and Kings: The Rise and Fall of Alexander McQueen and John Galliano,* and two Moomin mugs that she'd bought at the department store NK. I was about to ask if she didn't already have enough Moomin mugs, but luckily managed to bite my tongue in the nick of time. With an odd ceremoniousness she handed me the mugs and ordered me to put them into the dishwasher. I nodded like a butler and obediently took the Moomin mugs into the kitchen, where the weirdest feeling came over me.

You see, as I stood there basically stunned in front of the dishwasher, gazing at one of the Moomin mugs, which I later learned featured an original motif from Tove Jansson's chapter book *Moominpappa at Sea*, it was as though I was flung headlong and with full force into the scene depicted on the cup: Moominpappa sitting alone in the darkness—on what I would later come to see was a beach—staring into the blazing storm lantern in the foreground. In the background we get a glimpse of little Moomintroll (or perhaps even Moominmamma?) sleeping under an orange-and-white-checkered blanket in a makeshift tent.

I don't know why the image hypnotized me so. It was as though the Moomin motif was a perfect key to a door I'd never previously known, behind which an all-but magical sensation— a sensation that I'd perhaps been repressing for much of my life—lived in secret. I couldn't recall ever previously caring about the images on her Moomin mugs, but when it came to this *special* Moomin mug—which the producer Arabia named "Sleep Tight"—something extraordinarily remarkable had taken place. Something that could perhaps be explained by the fact that I had alcohol poisoning.

While Maria, who was now keeping me company in the kitchen, babbled on to herself about what we might have for dinner, I in turn stood, frozen on the spot with the Moomin mugs in my hands, completely overcome by a powerful sense of unreality. "They're really nice," I said, sounding like a teenage boy whose voice was just breaking; I immediately cleared my throat. "Of course they are!" Maria replied naively, before asking if it would be too boring to order pizzas from Cyrano as per. I didn't think so at all. "That sounds great," I assured her.—"Unless you've already eaten?"—"No, I haven't eaten anything today."—"Nothing at all?" she asked, concerned.—"Well, a piece of toast . . . and a few eggs, maybe." That was true. But it was even more true that the Moomin mug featuring the image from *Moominpappa at Sea* had well and truly hypnotized me with its profoundly original finesse. For it was indeed a really, really nice Moomin mug, I thought—and with complete conviction, at that. Moominpappa stoically keeping watch over his adventure-wearied family in the darkness—on the beach—through the night.

The other cup, however. The other cup I didn't find remotely as nice. In fact, the bottomless concentration that I'd devoted to the Moomin mug that I thought was really nice, the finest Moomin mug I'd ever encountered—a concentration that possessed an all-but *numinous* character, as though I was contemplating something sacred—was violently severed by the distaste verging on sheer discomfort—a *fanatical* discomfort!—provoked in me by the other Moomin mug, which I was holding in my other hand and hadn't formed any impression of before being positively engulfed by the image of

Moominpappa keeping watch on the beach, besides registering that it was mostly green in color.

In the middle of the other Moomin mug—entirely rationally entitled "Grass Green" by Arabia—Moomintroll stood, white and round and bowed like a coolie, his hand on one knee—perhaps preparing for complete *submission*—in front of a little black demon: a minidevil wearing a yellow headdress, and on top of that, two thin black horns.

I'm not entirely sure if I actually told Maria how much I disliked the green mug—whose image I later learned was taken from Jansson's 1957 comic *Moomin and the Martians*[*]—but I do remember being very surprised that she suddenly seemed a little offended for some reason.

It wouldn't be far-fetched to imagine that I may in fact have voiced some sort of judgment, perhaps even a very positive one, about the Moomin mug ("Sleep Tight") that I liked, a value judgment that could potentially have revealed how truly, truly little I, by contrast, rated the mug with the minidevil/Martian on it. In any case, I myself had been taken aback by the pure aversion I'd felt for the Moomin mug with the Martian on it—and so soon after feeling, in a melancholy moment of psychosis, the polar opposite for the first Moomin mug! As if that very illustration, from *Moominpappa at Sea*, which I hadn't yet read but would pull from Maria's bookshelf the very next day, was

---

[*]So what I'd initially taken to be a little devil was in fact no devil at all, just a little Martian who'd gotten lost after landing in the Moomin family's pristine garden.

speaking to me specifically about something potentially beau-tiful or meaningful that I carried within me—a veritable *pappa potential*, perhaps!—while the other mug had, with almost the same emotional intensity, stirred within me a diametrically op-posite reaction, overwhelmingly negative, that may have been somehow linked to my initial false interpretation of the image.

The intensity of my reaction to the Moomin mugs was, un-deniably, very odd. Though it's possible that I had previously, prior to this mystical event, managed to repress the fact that I had—without quite being able to put my finger on it—viewed the Moomin mugs as an indoctrination tool for the bourgeois moral order. They had stirred . . . indeed, they had stirred a sort of animosity within me. Perhaps that was why I'd been so happy when I got *the feels*—as they say—for the Moomin mug "Sleep Tight" and its atmospheric image from *Moominpappa and the Sea*?

What had previously held no appeal for me at all, these col-lectors' objects for Moomin devotees, symbols of what I had previously perceived as a bourgeois hegemony, all of a sud-den started to have an effect on me—one *more powerful*, I thought even then, more powerful than perhaps anyone else in Sweden!—and all this on the very day that I had come this close to killing Maria's Pomeranian, a bloody expensive little dog that I, truth be told, viewed as an archetypal (fetishistic) symbol of a social class that I both loved and despised, in ex-actly the same way that in my heart of hearts I at times both despised and loved that harmless little pooch.

Suddenly I realized that I was wittering on at myself about the merits of the "Sleep Tight" mug over the "Grass Green" one—that or I was simply just imagining that I was talking to myself. Apparently Maria had gone to take a shower, as I could hear the sounds coming from the bathroom: the clatter of water, Maria humming a Kent song. So maybe she wasn't all that mad after all? Had I perhaps just imagined that I'd said something about the Moomin mugs? It wasn't at all out of the question, given how fuzzy I was feeling. Obviously Maria could tell I'd drunk substantially more than the four or five beers I'd said I'd had. In all likelihood she could probably tell that I was still pretty drunk, or monumentally hungover at least.

When I finally managed to tear my eyes from the Moomin mugs, I saw that Molly was standing there watching me as I stood there, frozen, with the mugs in my hands. She gave me a slightly curious look, then went and lay down in her baby-blue basket under the kitchen table. Or in actual fact I suppose it was just her usual evening look, your average doggo look, but I'd probably gone and read something enigmatic into it. Once she'd positioned herself with her chin on the rim of the basket, she placed her paws over her muzzle and eyes, as usual. It looked both cute and a touch concerning. As though the mere sight of my crumbling figure had been enough to drive her to depression. I put the mugs into the dishwasher, took out a dishwasher tablet, slung it inside with a reckless abandon that almost shattered a wineglass, closed the door, and started a quick wash.

A little while later Maria came into the kitchen in her dressing gown and suggested we eat out at Cyrano, have a glass of wine, and catch up on the week that had been, but I couldn't help but be honest and confess I was just too shattered to sit in a restaurant. But if we did a takeaway? Yeah, that sounded all right, I thought, pretty great actually. Maria called and got dressed, we picked up the pizzas, and then watched a few episodes of *Better Call Saul*.

It was already eleven by the time we finally got to bed. In bed I told her about the big power cut that she'd missed. Tens of thousands of households in the central districts had lost power: Majorna, Masthugget, Högsbo, Långedrag, Haga, Torslanda, Biskopsgården—yes, even out on the archipelago there had been outages. "A fault in the order of one hundred and thirty kilovolts!" I said in a broad Gothenburg accent, imitating a dude from Göteborg Energi's power station who had spoken to the media. Maria laughed. That the fault was in the order of 130 kilovolts meant nothing to me.

Molly and I had been in my studio in Majorna when the power went, I told her. What had been really weird wasn't actually that the lights cut out around nine—leaving many people stuck in lifts around the city—as surprising as that had been—but what had happened just before. I'd been sitting in front of the computer reading a few WHO articles about the impact of heat waves on health while Molly lounged on the leather sofa, on the fleece blanket that she liked so much. Just a minute or so before the power cut out, plunging the entire block into darkness, Molly had started behaving oddly. All of a sudden she'd leapt up and thrown her head back and forth in a weird way, with a growl.

"What the fuck are you doing?" I'd asked, as it was already giving me the creeps. It was so bizarre that it was worrying. Still, she'd kept on doing it for maybe half a minute. But then the very instant the power went out she'd stopped!

"So she went back to normal then?"—"Yep, right back to normal! Obviously it was just a coincidence. And yet . . . yeah, it was still totally bizarre."

Maria was, as it happened, probably too young to remember the Tsunami disaster of 2004 well—I'd been no more than thirteen or fourteen myself—but perhaps she could still remember how oddly the animals had reacted before the big wave came?

"They ran away, didn't they?"—"Yeah, they must have sensed it all in some weird way."—"Maybe Molly's psychic?" I laughed, but when I realized Maria really meant it I swiftly corrected myself and agreed: "Yep, she might very well be psychic, actually—just like the elephants in Thailand."

9

DIALOGICAL ETHICS

The weeks after I'd all but snuffed Molly out were, as I recall, trying on a largely *spiritual* level. Because I'd made the snap decision to go completely alcohol-free for a while, I also sought, I suppose, a certain sustenance in religion, that is, Christianity, my own religion. Yes, it was *my* religion, without a doubt. But since my relationship with this religion was so diluted, as it were—since secular society had severed me from it (or it from me)—it felt way too pretentious to think of Christianity, this my own religion, in such possessive terms.

Anyway, I suppose I was a bit of a neophyte, especially since I'd more or less started to view myself as something of a "sober alcoholic." Besides displaying a newly awakened interest in the Bible, particularly the Gospels, the Sermon on the Mount, et

cetera, I'd also commandeered Maria's Wreath of Christ prayer
beads, which she never used anyway, and started wearing them
on my wrist. This surprised her a little. But I reassured her that
I'd simply just taken a liking to the bracelet and its glass beads
in different colors and sizes.

Truth be told, I suppose I considered wearing the former
bishop Martin Lönnebo's Wreath of Christ something of a
promise: *I would try to be a better person.* Thus the Wreath
of Christ became a daily and not overly indiscreet reminder
of my ambitions to pull my socks up, drink less (or not at all),
and become a more on the level, nonscuzzy, and authentically
grown-up person. Every now and then I also devoted myself to
what was supposedly the actual purpose of the bracelet, that's
to say peaceful reflections on the different aspects of the Christian faith, or life, that the beads represented.

The golden God bead symbolized the Lord and defined the
bracelet's beginning and end, its Alpha and Omega. The sandy
Desert bead sought to remind the wearer of life's trials, and
the endeavor to lead a "true" (or authentic) life. The bead of
Darkness, which was unsurprisingly black, represented death,
life's crises and setbacks. The dark-blue Carefree bead was supposed to call to mind the eternal now, freedom and an unbur-
dened mind. On Wikipedia I also read that the row of three
small white Secret beads could be filled with "secrets between
the individual and God," so I imagined that at least one of these
could house the "Molly Incident"—and my genuine guilt and
shame around it.

Anyway. I wanted to get my act together, I thought, "freshen myself up" inside. I borrowed books about Christian mysticism (and Sufism) from the library. And I started using nicotine patches—NiQuitin Clear 21 mg/24 hours—to get me off the nicotine pouches. My attitude to Molly changed; I started pampering the little pooch more. Maria said we'd clearly become "BFFs" during her *sejour* in Stockholm. Obviously she didn't realize the main reason why I was so "soppy" with the sprightly little thing was that I'd almost killed her. I even put a few hours aside to find out more about Molly's breed. On the Kennel Club website I read that the Zwergspitz/Pomeranian, like many other European breeds, is descended from the Stone Age peat dogs or *Canis familiaris palustris Rüthimeyer*. But way back when, their progenitor had, of course, been the wolf (however unlikely that seemed). Pomeranians captivated thanks to their beautiful, thick coat, which puffed out from the body because of their dense, woolly undercoat. They had a surprisingly robust, manelike ruff around the neck, and a bushy tail set "jauntily" over their back. Yes, that definitely sounded like Molly. Naturally she also had a foxy head with alert eyes and small, pointed, closely set ears, which, as with other Spitzes, gave her the übercute appearance so characteristic of this delightful breed.

A few *Not-So-Fluffy Facts About Pomeranians*: Queen Victoria fell head over heels for the breed in 1888 and immediately imported four Pomeranians from Italy, including Marco, a red sable male, and Gina, a white female. She was particularly fond of Marco, *who carried his tail over his back as though he owned the whole establishment.* Pomeranians were also, I read online, "survivors." Alongside the 2,240 people who stepped aboard the fated ocean liner RMS *Titanic*, there also numbered twelve dogs. Of these only three survived, a Pekingese and two Pomeranians.

Apparently artists, too, had a certain faiblesse for the animal. Mozart dedicated one of his arias to his dog Pimperl. Chopin had been inspired to compose the "Minute Waltz" (or "*Valse du petit chien*") by the sight of his friend's pets chasing their own tails. Michelangelo had supposedly had his Pomeranian sitting on a silk cushion beside him while he painted the Sistine Chapel in Rome.

The July days post "Molly Incident" were also marked by a prolonged blazing heat. The sun tirelessly persisted in corroding your face whenever you were outside. It truly was like living in a more southerly nation. The lawns were all yellow and frazzled, and the hot air still hung, static or tremulous, between the rows of buildings. Since Maria still had some weeks of holiday left before she started her summer job at the Linnéstaden library in town, she was often at home when I got back from work after lunch. It wasn't uncommon for the place to be injuriously hot. Opening the windows didn't help, and electric fans were basically impossible to get your hands on; they were sold out everywhere. Maria, for understandable reasons, wasn't exactly bundled up in clothes in these days, and nor was I for that matter, but she did also have a tendency—from my perspective—to push her seminakedness nerve-rackingly far. She would often strut past provocatively with an annoying little grin on her face, clad in only her sportily feminine yet also fascist-vibe-emitting black-and-white bra (a *bralette*) and thong of the same brand (Emporio Armani), something that unfailingly tended to attract my full attention after a while. On several of these occasions I felt compelled—indeed, more or less prevailed upon!—to reprimand and punish the shameless vixen for her coquettish exhibitionism. (Incidentally, on these occasions I made sure to *take off* my Wreath of Christ—temporarily suspending my piety—so that that particular Christian fetish wouldn't be tainted by excessively indecent deeds.)

Because Maria had previously insinuated that I had some sort of fixation on her flat chest, I increasingly took to taunting her (though obviously with a glint in my eye) for her insufficient (or else possibly "disgusting" or "pathetic") mammary development. On one occasion, I'd taken a firm grip around the nape of the shameless tomboy's neck, then roughly escorted the recalcitrant wench to the sofa, where I proceeded to push her down onto her stomach and tease her a little as she lay there with her petite buns in the air, but, just as I was about to insert one finger or perhaps even two into her rosy bumhole, her phone rang, and she (perhaps without quite thinking, or possibly as a sort of subconscious act of defiance) quickly snatched it up and took the call! When I heard the sober (or perhaps more completely mundane) greeting "Hi, Dad!" I wiped my fingers off on her thong in disappointment, went into the kitchen, and put on a cup of Nespresso, since I'd immediately caught the drift that she wouldn't be ending the call anytime soon.

Afterward Maria told me that her father had been waxing lyrical, indeed, had been way too excited, she claimed, for her to have had any chance of ending the call once it had started. Apparently both her father and mother were now members and shareholders of Bro Hof—whatever that was. Maria informed me that Bro Hof was an exclusive golf club located around forty minutes from central Stockholm by car.

So anyway, Carl-Johan had asked her to let me know that he really looked forward to hitting a round with me at some point, perhaps at the end of August, when we had planned to visit them for a weekend. Fact was, I was completely mind blown when Maria later mentioned that they had put a few hundred thousand kronor into the partnership. But as time wore on I would also come to feel increasingly excited at the prospect of getting to play at one of Sweden's and perhaps northern Europe's best golf courses, even though it was years since I'd swung a club.

Of course, Maria's exhibitionism wasn't to blame for the fact that I was, by this point, much more slack at keeping up my routine of writing from one to five every day. The villains in the drama were none other than me, myself, and I. It had just all gotten too much. Way too much. Too many nights with Johannes at Plankan, Eli's Corner, or Oceanen. Nights that had successively diminished my sense of responsibility, made me more slovenly, and—yes, perhaps even stupid. In short, I'd been unable to summon a work ethic à la Stephen King or Jan Guillou, and perhaps—I thought bitterly—I never would be able to. The longer the heat wave wore on, the more I had increasingly more or less fallen off the wagon (if it's possible to fall off a wagon more or less, that is). But I had no intention of blaming that on the heat wave, at least not seriously. If I'd dropped my daily writing, quit working as a professional writer—which I had—then, well, that was my own choice. My own fate.

Though I considered myself mature enough not to point any fingers at Johannes (neither for the "Molly Incident," nor for any other setback in my admittedly rather uneventful and not especially remarkable life), and though he had de facto been something of a booze brother—and perhaps an enabler—through that summer's hot afternoons and evenings, I was now nevertheless starting to critically reflect on our friendship. There was no doubt that I viewed him—this friend who had increasingly started to bomb me with links to YouTube conspiracy theory clips and bizarre alt-right memes that he'd found on 4chan—as a somewhat more extreme and fundamentalist character than myself, *though I didn't rule out the fact that I, too, was extreme and fundamentalist in a way, since I— clearly—enjoyed his company so much.*

Shouldn't I have had a set of more *normative* pals? Sure, I did go out with Maria, and every now and then with her friends, too, I reasoned, and I saw my pretty normative colleagues every morning, but by and large I had—in recent months— nevertheless become more and more attached to Johannes— indeed, perhaps almost *dependent* on his company (something that may also have had something to do with my, I suspect, burgeoning alcohol consumption).

In a (possibly half-hearted) attempt to broaden my social network, one day I got in touch with an old high-school class- mate, Jacob—who was now Father Jacob. Since I didn't feel like getting the whole Blood-of-Christ spiel (which I guessed should be around 12 percent alcohol anyway) at his Catholic clergy house, I suggested meeting at Junggrens Café for a cof- fee. With Father Jacob (who was, as such, an entirely different person from the Jacob I'd mooched down Andra Långgatan with in the noughties) it took surprisingly little time to rein- state our former friendly familiarity, and I immediately started describing my deliberations over whether to write about my thinking around *debased*, *destroyed*, and *demolished* rooms, those wildly *spiraling* and, I described, severely *derailed* and increasingly *degenerate* rooms that occasionally, I confessed, gave me nightmares.

Father Jacob had, logically enough, interpreted these spaces as representations of a sort of mental or spiritual darkness, and, since I was interested in literature and had started to develop an interest in Christian mysticism at that (as I'd told him I had), he recommended the Carmelite nun Teresa of Ávila's *The Interior Castle*, which apparently described rooms of the sort that I was after; filled with snakes and rats and the like. In addition to this, Father Jacob also recommended (albeit for other reasons) John of the Cross's *Dark Night of the Soul* and *Ascent of Mount Carmel*, which he suspected I might enjoy, if for nothing else than their indisputable literary qualities.

Obviously I received these recommendations gratefully, and I even jotted them down in my notebook, but it would be a few years before I would actually take the time to look up these mystics in earnest, perhaps above all because this (and also other) attempts to expand my almost nonexistent network of more normative friends wouldn't bear all that much fruit. The reunion with Father Jacob had generally proved satisfactory, I can probably say as much, since I'd very much appreciated the (in both senses) sober and intellectually stimulating conversation, but at the same time I realized that Father Jacob—who actually not only wasn't the old Jacob anymore, but, as he, Father Jacob, put it himself, was now a link in an almost two-thousand-year-old chain of men of God—was beyond hanging out in a truly relaxed (and unaffected) ongoing way. I also struggled to see how more frequent meetups with Father Jacob wouldn't basically lead to a risk of me being more or less indoctrinated with Catholic propaganda—especially since I knew that I was enormously suggestible and therefore vulnerable given my current (perhaps "newly spiritual") quest.

Anyway, after a while I could reach no other conclusion than that Johannes, despite his radical non-PC-ness, really was the only male (and intellectual) friend that I truly enjoyed hanging out with at the time. In his company I had also, with time, pretty much detoxed myself from a true need for the socializing influence of more normative people.

At my so-called day job, the heat wave was—as usual—the main focus just then. Now that we were starting to near the end of July, we could predict with some certainty that the heat wave would be the hottest ever recorded in Sweden, in addition to the forest fires being the most serious in the country's modern history. Soon the government would even be distributing 1.2 billion kronor to the farmers who'd been hardest hit by the prolonged drought. Some of them had been forced to feed their livestock bananas due to the alarming scarcity of ordinary hay. Incidentally, on July 30, Ringhals 2 Nuclear Power Plant would be taken offline, as the waters of the Kattegat had gotten too warm to cool the reactor; something truly unprecedented.

My boss, Claes, was still extremely flustered yet also, I suspect, *happy*. If nothing else, the whole thing had livened him up a bit, at least—and me, too, I suppose. The heat wave and Action Plan Ra had certainly created a few unexpected events, at a workplace where these tended to be relatively few and far between. For example, one morning Claes had come racing into my office and, panting, had pretty much shouted at me:

"Have you seen the cars!?" I had not. "You've got to see the cars the MSB have given us!" After that he had all but shoved me out onto the street, where two brand-spanking-new, souped-up Toyota Land Cruiser 105s were parked. I was impressed; there was something unquestionably powerful about the enormous carriages.

"They've got four-wheel drive," said Claes.

"Obviously!" I replied.

"And, as you can see, they've also got these . . . *light arrangements*," he said and pointed, clearly meaning the row of LED spotlights mounted on the front of the roof, and the off-road lights on the grille.

"Our very own work vehicles!" he said proudly.

He was quite simply beside himself. Still, I must say it cheered me to see him so extremely chipper. The simple truth (that I assume Claes had temporarily chosen to overlook) was that the Unit probably wouldn't actually get any great use out of the vehicles. After all, our work was mainly to provide information. Indeed, the bulk of our operations revolved around the analysis, management, and review of consequences that (when it came to that year's heat wave) understandably couldn't yet be summarized. Clearly we couldn't hold every swimmer's hand, protect them from drowning or from getting a Vibrio infection. It didn't fall to us to extinguish the forest fires. And we certainly had no mandate to arrest or fine those who defied the fire bans that by this point were in place across the entire country.

None of that prevented Claes from milking Action Plan Ra to the full. At the very least, it was clear that those mighty work vehicles (which I wasn't alone in suspecting would imminently have to be returned, seeing as they should be able to do more good in Congo or somewhere) had put him out of action for a few days. He didn't even notice that, overnight, Camilla had once again started dressing in a completely respectable manner. For the rest of us, however, this didn't go unnoticed. It amused me to see Solveig immediately welcome her into the fold again with open arms. Her warm, motherly gaze was back. Camilla had returned to her gray, Lutheran-informed flock. The carnival was over.

By the way, I did get a memorable opportunity to ride in one of the emergency vehicles one day, after I'd been hobbling around like a more or less handicapped person all morning due to some terrible postworkout stiffness (in my legs). The day before, Maria and I had gone bowling with a few of her mates. By then Lasse had been back at work for a few days, slightly pale and drawn at first, and everyone had been happy to see him again. Since he and Claes had a special bond—primarily due to their shared admiration for Ulf Lundell[*]—Lasse had immediately been presented with responsibility for one of the vehicles. An idea that I couldn't help but think wasn't all that well thought through on Claes's part. Especially since it was

---

[*]Ulf Gerhard Lundell (born November 20, 1949). A Swedish writer, poet, songwriter, and artist who occupies an undeniably Springsteenian position in the Swedish canon of songwriting and rock poetry.

glaringly obvious that Lasse had spent the summer in a psychiatric facility.

Anyway, the team had just eaten lunch and I'd been about to head home for the day when Lasse suddenly offered me a lift in one of the new 4×4s. I'd expressed a certain hesitancy, but Claes had immediately supported Lasse's suggestion and emphatically declared that it might just be a superb idea, given that I could hardly walk. Which was quite true. How had I even made it into work that morning? he asked. And then he added—which I'd found extremely strange (and slightly concerning)—that Lasse was *a fucking good driver, actually*. In short, I felt like I had no choice but to accept the offer.

And so it was.

I was really just going back to Maria's place on Linnégatan, but Lasse suggested taking a little detour, if I wasn't against—so I could see what a Land Cruiser could really do. Since I had zero plans of sitting at my writing desk between one and five, I had nowhere I had to be, so Lasse started setting course for the center of town at an alarming speed. Pretty soon after, he turned down the radio to low and started telling me that he'd been totally fucking devastated by the sudden death of his father. They hadn't been exactly tight, he said, but still, "there was a lot there." He was feeling much better now, he assured me. I offered my condolences, as one should, and thought it was nice (and perhaps a little odd) that he seemed to have so much trust in me.

He told me that he'd read Gunnar Ekelöf's *Ferry Song* when he was in the facility. Well, once he'd started to feel a little better, that is. His girlfriend had brought him a few books that he'd had lying on his nightstand. Once he could finally start expressing himself around what he was reading (and other things), the psychiatrist in charge of the place had sent him home. Had I read *Ferry Song*? Yes, I had. "It feels like Sweden's started to forget Ekelöf," he said. "As though She repressed." I didn't get quite what he meant there, but replied that "the poets of our day might not really have access to the same . . . well, well-articulated earnestness," hoping that my words would fall on fertile ground. "Exactly!" Lasse said. That was it. There was no depth in this fucking society anymore. The poets of the day were basically mostly . . . uh, like sloppy slam poets?

For fifteen, twenty minutes we drove around aimlessly, crisscrossing through the center—and it was a strange and, I must say, almost filmic experience. Both Lasse's melancholy and the impression that I'd had that he was still medicated had briefly disappeared, and his eyes had shone with a crystal-clear glint of enthusiastic concentration.

In Lasse's inner world, I speculated afterward, there had per-haps been something almost Lundellian about flouting traffic laws in the oversize service vehicle that the MSB had presum-ably basically given us in error; as though we, in an act of teen-age rebellion, had taken the silencer off our scooters and split from an oppressive family home, sending the dust and dirt fly-ing behind us down all the world's roads.

Once Lasse had slowed down and brought the car to a slow crawl outside Scandinavium arena, as though we were on a stakeout or something, like a cop car, without thinking I'd started telling him about the so-called Molly Incident, and, to my own surprise, I held nothing back. On that day I'd basically bumped off Maria's dog because of my drinking, and, in my own words, I'd been afraid of myself. Worried. I didn't cry or anything, at least I don't think so, I probably wouldn't say that I did, but at several points in my confession my voice did catch in my throat.

When I'd finished my account, I realized that Lasse, without me really noticing, had parked the car outside Valhallabadet Swimming Hall. Suddenly I felt a hand on my shoulder and glanced over at him nervously, out of fear that he'd be giving me an overly judgy look, but all I saw was humanity and acceptance. He didn't need to say a thing. I realized that he'd taken my story as a token of trust. "Now let's get you home," he said softly, then started up the car.

The next day I found out that the government had decided to give Region Västra Götaland a supplementary budget of several million, which according to Claes meant that the County Administrative Board could extend my employment by at least a year, after which I might even be able to go full-time, if I wanted. My job was thus saved and potentially doubled. Claes reckoned we could now seriously discuss whether I could do that registrar training in autumn that we'd been looking at, which could in turn give me an even stronger foothold at the Unit. This made me happy, since if I could hang in there at the Unit—where I'd already demonstrated I was a "meaningful and valued member of the team," to quote *Penguins of Madagascar*—then my livelihood would be secured and my life would become even more respectable and, yes, perhaps even supernormative on the whole. Still, I couldn't help but wonder how truly gray and mediocre such a nine-to-five existence ran the risk of becoming. The trap that the "40-40-40 con" might still potentially entail risked slamming resolutely shut behind me: 40 hours of work per week for 40 years of my life, then 40 percent of my salary in my pension. Sure, on the other hand I would get a *workplace pension*, but still.

If I was expected to work full time as a document controller, I could well and truly kiss my plans of writing more regularly and at exact times every day for the rest of my life, à la Stephen King, goodbye. With a full-time job, the laborious process of writing a novel, *if I was even capable of that, that is*, could take . . . well, maybe decades? But it also hit me, in my overwrought and newly awakened religiosity, that this news could be part of an all-out divine *intervention*.

Perhaps God himself was of the opinion that I shouldn't write anything at all.

Indeed, even if I had by this point well and truly fucked up my routine of parking myself at my desk (or Maria's kitchen table) between one and five, Monday to Sunday, and even if

God was perhaps of the opinion that I shouldn't write another line, sentence, or phrase of literature for the rest of my life, I couldn't let go of my fantasies of completing something with Houellebecq as a protagonist. For even though the thought of writing in general, and my obsession with my lack of competence in particular (when it came to writing a comprehensible story from A to Z, or a so-called *straightforward* narrative), truly tormented me at times, my Houellebecq fantazising (or perhaps more *unconditional daydreaming*) was still something quite different—something that on the grand scale of things felt like nothing but flights of fancy or escapism.

By the way, I still suspected Johannes had been right in his forthright (verging on humiliating) remarks. I mean, it was completely obvious—even to myself—that I did indeed have a psychological need to *impersonate* Houellebecq. That being said, I was not prepared to truly believe, as Johannes had claimed, that I was someone who refused to live or was simply incapable of living *in reality* and had no experience of true *suffering*. (Besides, physical suffering—pain—was, according to Peterson, the only thing that humankind could agree on as being something essentially true. Pain simply can't help but seem more real than anything else. A phenomenological reality.)

Or did I simply have no body? Was I not body? Was that what he had meant? That if I didn't have a body in which physical suffering could be situated, I therefore had no possibility of living in (or even cognizing) the so-called real world? Despite obviously wanting to dismiss this as rubbish, I realized there could be a certain truth to his argument. Didn't both Maria and I basically live pretty much overly comfortable middle-class lives? At least in most respects.

Friction-free lives. Bloodless lives. Lives without violence; without pain. With few (*extremely* few) external threats, and few (though not necessarily nonexistent) internal threats. It wasn't as though we had any enemies. Our relationship was free from *affects*. Our conflicts were banal, few (*extremely* few, actually), and quickly over and done with. We were, I thought, *soft*. Young (relatively speaking) and . . . well, perhaps *blunt*—kind of softened up, I mean—around the edges.

Invulnerable in our very, uh, immaturity?

If we weren't *realistic*—weren't fully rooted in reality's soil of true suffering—wasn't that also due to an absence of suffering, the essential lightness of our senses and respective natures? And was I not, I argued, pretty happy with all of that on the whole? A permanently tetchy Maria would have been a terrifying and unbearable prospect; I couldn't even imagine how such a Maria specimen would manifest herself. Besides, I wasn't so afraid of loneliness that I would put up with a relationship that put me through such tests. And even if we were perhaps lambs instead of wolves, soft wool in place of fangs, surely that didn't automatically make us NPCs?

But was that even what Johannes had implied that night? Had he seriously meant that all women were *non-playable characters*? I couldn't remember.

The thought that I personally might possibly be an NPC actually felt pretty satisfying, in a way. Did it not basically imply (to think as I thought Houellebecq might think) a certain chance of actually being happy? A real chance to live a happily timid, stupid, and (lap)doglike existence? If such a potential soullessness, I argued, also brought with it the possibility to harness the *perfect* level of stupidity with which to produce middlebrow literature for a wider readership between the hours of one and five each day, I would be very much down for it. Indeed, even if Johannes's NPC guff was empty words and no more, I still felt attacked—as, by the way, I've already admitted. It wasn't at all impossible that I didn't get what reality was, that I didn't live in the real world, since I wasn't personally acquainted with suffering. On the other hand, suffering certainly wasn't anything I felt any serious desire to get to know better.

In any event, I started sketching out another chapter on Houellebecq in my mind, one that would pick up where the earlier one (Chapter Six) left off—or, no, it would begin the day after the French writer was paid a visit by Police Inspector Grayson. The protagonist would obviously be hungover. Anything else seemed unthinkable. But that Houellebecq himself would be someone to simply grin and bear it as some form of punishment, as it were, didn't seem all that realistic, and so, I fantasized, it was obviously completely logical that the first thing he would do upon waking would be to go into the kitchen and uncork another bottle of white.

With ease I pictured him hauling himself into the living room, filling a wineglass to the brim, and flopping onto the sofa like the living dead for a while, perhaps even lolling. His wife-to-be, Lysis, would still be away for another few days with Rex the dog at her friend's place in Marseille. Once he had perked up slightly, the controversial writer would perhaps think about how he missed his fiancée's "Confucian presence" (or something of that ilk), but the thought of this, his (*authentic*) longing, would soon be overtaken by the semigenuine inkling that that very thought, or feeling, perhaps—indeed, a completely *authentic* feeling—might perchance express, well, if not quite pure Sinophobia then at least a lack of political correctness. Or, no, he probably *wouldn't* think that.

Would he perhaps tally up what he could recall of the previous night? Yes. Much of it was, of course, a little hazy. It would be best, therefore, to take it all in chronological order. The conversation with Grayson he would certainly remember, at least in broad strokes.

Consequently, he would cringe slightly about that bloody rant of his about Batman and Robin. Christ, he'd fucking *bloviated* about those masquerading shit-for-brains! It wasn't impossible that he might even have come across as . . . well, a bit of a closet gay or something. But surely it would be highly unreasonable for Grayson to think that he, Michel Houellebecq—whose

heterosexual identity nevertheless presented as completely un-
ambiguous and on top of that particularly well documented—
would have tried to make a pass at him? Nope, he should forget
all that. The inspector had let himself be coaxed into drinking
maybe two glasses of wine. That much he remembered. But
when had he actually left his apartment in Les Olympiades?

Anyway, the writer had been woken up later, around eight
p.m., by his neighbor Caroline—who had a master's degree in
art history from École Normale Supérieure but made her living
from the properties she had inherited from her father, which
allowed her to devote herself to her passion of practicing and
teaching Latin American dance—who had called and asked to
speak to Lysis, as apparently she hadn't been answering her
phone all day. The writer had explained that Lysis was in Marseille and was probably busy with her lady friend, who was a
dog acupuncturist.

Caroline (incidentally, one of a total of 6,221 French girls
born in 1979 to be given that name) had laughed heartily. After
a short, spiritual conversation he had had the good sense to invite her over for a glass of wine, but at the same time he didn't
neglect to warn her that he was already verging on "a completely asocial degree of inebriation." With a laugh she'd said:
"I can hear that well enough!" and then taken him up on the
offer, and Houellebecq would truly be able to picture, in his
well-practiced inner eye, I thought, the not-half-bad brunette,
looks-wise, practically *twinkling* with her entire being.

Then he would possibly remember them sitting at the white marble slab of the kitchen island—he had cracked open a few packs of *antipasti*—while discussing an esoteric book that Caroline had read. But what was the title? It wasn't Huysmans, at any rate. That much he would have remembered. Someone else. Perhaps Villiers de L'Isle-Adam? Though did he really write esoteric stuff?

For some inscrutable reason, after a while they had gotten onto discussing *What Is Ancient Philosophy?*, by historian of philosophy Pierre Hadot. A dispute had arisen after the writer claimed that the "Socratic" dialogue that Hadot describes could never occur, generally speaking, between men and women—for "a range of more or less controversial reasons."

Caroline had rolled her eyes, and in his own inebriated state the writer had exclaimed, verging on the overly aggressive: "Oh don't roll your eyes like that!" and Caroline had (with perhaps mainly *feigned* anger) wittily replied: "Oh fuck you! I'll do whatever the fuck I want!" Whereupon Houellebecq had instinctively recoiled slightly. "I know you're probably just going to give me a whole heap of bullshit, anyway," Caroline would perhaps add.

"No, I'm not going to bullshit . . ." he would reply, with a warm yet wounded voice. ". . . I promise!"

"Hmm. Well explain what you mean then."

"In essence, it perhaps isn't any more complicated than . . . well, that *desire* gets in the way of a Socratic dialogue between a man and a woman, and, because that desire gets in the way, it prevents them from transcending their own subjectivity. To-gether they are incapable of surrendering to the rational re-quirements of such a logical discourse, of *logos*. The quality of the dialogue will therefore be sabotaged by desire or libido. And libido in this case needn't simply be reduced to sexual pleasure, to cock and cunt; one can see it (à la Jung) rather as an entire battery of unconscious desires: the desire for the (good) father, the desire for the (good) mother, et cetera.

"Moreover, the woman will be completely guarded (or devout), especially these days; she won't want to end up in a subordinate position in what she imagines is a battle for the *construction* of the truth, and her compulsive antagonism will become . . . well, simply much more important to her than *logos*. The masculine dialogue partner will, without exception, be viewed as an incarnation of the unwaveringly evil patriar-chy. The discourse becomes a power struggle. But the Socratic dialogue cannot be about power, no, Caroline, it cannot be a struggle, no tug-of-war, for then Socratic dialogue it is not.

"These days," Houellebecq would go on, "these hypothetical dialogues between man and woman are preemptively disqualified due to postmodernism's fixation on power relationships. Which is why I'm assured that that Socratic dialogue per se—in Hadot's or perhaps rather Plato's idealistic sense—has and will never take place between a man and a woman." (The author wobbled slightly precariously on his barstool.) "If one can't envisage a dialogue ever revolving around something other than power . . . well, no form of mutual understanding can *ever* be achieved."

"Hmm. You really *are* very drunk."

"Yes, perhaps, but this definitely isn't bullshit. Definitely not!"

"Maybe not. There's a kernel of truth to your argument. A so-called Socratic dialogue between men and women could be hindered by . . . well, libido as you put it, or, rather, by man's asinine horniness and by the *ressentiment* of the modern, semieducated woman. But let's say you don't know if the person you're talking to is in fact a man or woman—kind of like a Turing test or a 'Chinese room'—would a Socratic discourse be completely impossible then? You wouldn't know if the person you're speaking to is a man or a woman. You wouldn't know if they are white or Black. As such, you should be able to focus fully on *logos*, on the identification of reason (which is neither fully male nor female)—indeed, on God, you would be able to focus fully on God, or at least on what one might regard as Western society's *ethos*. So is the problem then solved . . . ?"

"Hmm. Yes, perhaps . . . I suppose."

"Surely even you can see that men and women, historically speaking, have had many important and highly rational conversations with each other? Just take Socrates's dialogue with Diotima!* Though admittedly, come to think of it, perhaps that dialogue wasn't a Socratic discourse in Hadot's sense. After all, Diotima was presenting the concept of Platonic love; she was instructing.

---

*Plato. (2003). *The Symposium* (translated by Christopher Gill; revised edition). Penguin Classics. This dialogue was originally written around 385–370 BC.

(And she instructed *with* power, I think, not in order to win it. A power conferred upon her by women and men in a culture that understood, felt, and respected Woman's mind, Woman's being.) She would hardly be amused if her pupil brutally refuted her. That would be downright blasphemous, would it not?"

"Hmm. Well, yes, of course."

"After all, Socrates is young at this point. One would assume he has a deep respect for this woman's authority. Like for a wise mother. Therefore, this isn't a case of discursive reasoning subject to logos—no, Diotima's words *are* logos. She *is* wise. A manifestation of wisdom. And, Michel, listen now, she is also a manifestation of the *consciousness* that transcends gender, that transcends gender and race, age and social standing. She isn't a nonwise person like Socrates, who, incidentally, was well aware of his nonwisdom, of his position as neither insane (which is what those who believe themselves wise in fact are) nor wise. He is a *daimon*, as Hadot writes. A mix of the divine and human. As such he is *atopotatos*, and everything he creates is *aporia*. That is, something foreign, *mal placé*, almost distracted and dissonant . . . Hmm. Yes, he is 'problematic,' just like you, Michel. For that is how people generally see you, no?"

"Hah! Socrates is 'problematic.'"

"What I like about your reasoning, even if it does, in its entirety, ooze a certain *tragique*, is that it supports my own belief that modern woman has totally lost sight of characters like Diotima. How many people know of Demeter and Persephone, nowadays? The Eleusinian Mysteries? The ladies who go to see tragedies like *Medea* and *Agamemnon* at the theater have already got one foot in the grave. Their misogyny is *trans-* or even *pansexually* internalized, if one can say as much. For the majority of today's women, the Great Mother doesn't exist; no one wants Woman's existence to have any sort of connection to the *chthonic*, to aspects of the Underworld or to the principle that Woman can be both that which gives life and that which takes it away. Woman cannot be death's right hand, and she certainly can't be Death itself. She can't even have any connection to moral ambivalence anymore. She can't represent nature's cosmic uncertainty. She can't have any ties to the maenads who tore Orpheus to shreds. Woman's chthonic power is taboo.

"Indeed, even if I don't entirely agree with you, I do believe that, generally speaking, this could result in what you're describing. That's to say that the woman refuses to listen to the man for her own chauvinistic reasons. In other words, most women don't want any Socratic dialogue whatsoever with people of the opposite sex; they would be capable of one, certainly, but they simply haven't the inclination. A true discursive encounter is thus denied them, perhaps, by the superstructures of neoliberal capitalism."

"Hmm. Yes, you might just be right! . . . They haven't the inclination. Those little lives. As it were. But then perhaps . . ." (Houellebecq wobbled on his barstool again, and this time came very close to falling off it.) ". . . perhaps that's also why the little cunts don't get all that wet from playing with . . . well, with cars . . . or little plastic Uzis."

"Oh for fuck's sake, Michel!" snorted Caroline. "Yes, that was *exactly* what I was meaning, truly. You really are a terrible listener. It's hardly strange that *your* Socratic dialogues with women are so few or nonexistent in number. Look no further than yourself!"

"Huh?" The author was . . . well, pretty out of it.

As such, when it came to the Socratic dialogue, they wouldn't get all that much further. Caroline was no doubt riled by the author's mental absence, of course, but not exaggeratedly so, for above all she pitied the aged man, so after a while they moved on to matters much better suited to the author's almost laughably stratospheric degree of intoxication. Besides, Caroline was amused by the uninhibited voracity with which the author started to help himself to the Italian medley (incidentally, of very high quality). At one point Caroline got it into her head to insist on teaching the author a few dance steps. This he remembered clearly. Caroline was truly a sight to behold in her tight black cocktail dress and high-heeled shoes. *A classic woman!* he had perhaps thought. The dancing had gone decently enough, one might say, at least until the author had slipped and fallen pretty badly. Not in such a way as to break anything. No, his left arm didn't hurt all that much anymore (I pictured him giving it a rub as he sat there on the sofa). But in any case it wasn't good.

At some point in the evening, pretty late on, he couldn't remember when exactly, Caroline had thanked him and gone back to her Angora cat named Dexter. After which the author had dozed off in front of the TV news, a bag of frozen peas clutched to his elbow.

I guess that would be it, I imagined, all that he would remember from the previous night. He would then take a glug of wine. Heave a great sigh. Then another glug. And another. He would notice that the sun was shining like a fucking chump even today. Yes, what would this shitty day have in its rotten store? Nothing but shit, presumably. Hence nothing of central import. He would perhaps write something. Anything. A little poem. Or two. Immediately he would feel *a complete indifference*. A truly, well, to him surprisingly unpleasant feeling. According to Orthodox Catholicism, indifference in itself— especially the mental state of *total* indifference—I imagined Houellebecq thinking—could be defined as something with *demonic* properties, or was it more of an actual *real* demon, so to speak? A *de facto demon* of pure indifference; irremissibly bred in the primordial flames of, oh yes, indifference itself. Indeed. Though surely *it*, this entity, would or should be possible to exorcise like almost any other demon, right?

10

NORMATIVITY'S BARRIER

On Maria's initiative, the time had once again come for us to have Agnes and Otto over for dinner. Four months had passed since their last visit, and it was indisputable that a whole lot had happened since then. Mostly nothing to write home about. I'd been on the brink of losing my job, only to find out I'd kept it, and would perhaps get even more to do than before: that is, more day job (working hours) than I really wanted.

I had also, upon realizing the value of fixed routines, finally gotten going with my novel, only to fall back out of the saddle before I knew it, and by this point I didn't know if I actually wanted to get back in. Not that I believed I was incapable of writing one—I was completely convinced I could write some

sort of novel—but I still hadn't quite managed to shake the feeling that I was completely incompetent when it came to realizing a work—aligned with genre fiction's formal requirements
of language and the like—that could appeal to a wider readership or (ideally) a so-called educated public (if such a public
still existed?).

It's possible that I was in a sort of limbo of melancholy ambivalence. While mourning the possibility of reaching a mass
readership, I did nevertheless slowly start to accept that I might
perhaps one day manage to create something that I at least considered *real* literature. By this point I'd definitely started to let
go of my incompetence fixation slightly, and even though my
novel project was on ice, I'd still kept up my so-called Houellebecq meditations, or Houellebecq emulations. In a matter of
weeks I'd accumulated at least thirty or so pages.

As I had no desire to sit around at the pub anymore, I was
seeing Johannes less and less often, but I'd still sent him some
of my texts via email. He most liked an episode in which the
French author, on his fiancée Lysis's suggestion, sets some
hours aside to write a children's book in which a large pack of
animals (wild and tame) present a potpourri of different career
pathways for children. It could be an illustrated chapter book,
but it was heading more toward being a picture book with just
a few lines on each page, possibly written in verse. Lysis felt
that the profits should be donated in full to the Société Protec-
trice des Animaux (SPA), the oldest animal rights association
in France, which was founded in the mid-nineteenth century.

The professions that would be represented, I reasoned Houellebecq would reason, should be relatively concrete, while overly abstract occupations, such as market analysts, copywriters, or curators (in the art world) would presumably go right over the target group's heads. Certain vocations would be completely unthinkable to include, or at least highly inappropriate, such as prostitutes, priests, or hit men, though I supposed that those were mostly "professions" within quotation marks.

Anyway, the writer envisaged a gang of surly polecats (in diving suits) cleaning the drains of a big, blushing sow who stood there nervously rubbing her chapped hooves. A brown Labrador who was president (a nod to Macron!) being served chamomile tea by a penguin (a butler), at whom the statesman didn't even deign to cast a glance. A blasé (but nonetheless professional) crab styling the hair of a self-righteous poodle—who, on another page, would in turn be selling cashmere jumpers to a Russian nouveau-riche silver fox. A doped-up boxer tiling an exceedingly grateful rhinoceros's bathroom. A frantically stamping hare massaging the hefty back of a blissful (sacred?) cow. And so on.

Houellebecq thought, I thought, that the book could perhaps be entitled *Animals Help Each Other*. But could it truly be classed as *help* (in the more altruistic sense of the word) if the animals were taking payment? Perhaps not. Alternative titles like *Animals at Each Other's Service* or *Animals Serving Each Other* would probably arouse rather peculiar associations. But obviously this would be no Marxist children's book! Certainly not. Completely ignoring the hierarchies of the animal kingdom was hardly in the cards. It would be tendentious to have a servile tiger polishing the cloven hooves of a little sheep, a stupid little herd animal, especially if the former would also be forced to apologize for its historic "tiger privilege."

What else had happened in those months? The key event, surely, must be said to have been the fact that I'd all but set up Molly's tragic demise thanks to my—truth be told—unbridled drinking? Yes, it probably was. With no thought to the consequences, I had shut down my *prefrontal cortex* and become as rash as a four-year-old. And, as I've perhaps already mentioned, such little kids couldn't be allowed to play with a dog like Molly. Yet I had allowed myself to regress to that burly lout! A lengthy period of sobriety was completely essential.

It was possibly with this specific baggage that I—in weeks gone by—had forced myself to revise my previous attitude to Agnes's and Otto's, our much-anticipated guests, own pet history.

Unlike my basically secret Molly Incident, their Frodo-the-cat equivalent had been laid out for all to see; they hadn't kept it to themselves, quite the opposite. Me, I'd kept everything from Maria—a fact that undeniably chafed a little on my conscience. Still, my more immediate shame had eroded with time; wasn't I, perhaps, I occasionally reasoned, making a bit of a meal of the Molly Incident? Was I perhaps exaggerating this relatively trivial mishap to make my own life seem more interesting than it actually was? Yes, I did think so at times.

But my conclusion regarding the Molly Incident was—and would also remain—that it was, in short, a serious and anything but negligible misdemeanor on my part. Indeed, it was only after the Molly Incident that I seriously came to understand what Frodo's disappearance might really have meant to Agnes and Otto. Swooping in at the eleventh hour and "saving" that beer-stinky dog from the laundry basket had undeniably been a genuine eye-opener for me.

My conscience wasn't clear—oh no—and it was probably to this that one could trace my intention, as that evening's host, to be a genuinely far more sympathetic and empathic person than the version of myself that Agnes and Otto had met a few months before. I'd even suggested we go all out: pull out all the stops, make a real night of it. Therefore, we would be serving Toast Skagen to start, entrecôte with a homemade béarnaise and potato croquettes for the main, and crème brûlée for dessert. I was to take care of the starters, and Maria the rest. I bought the prawns for the Skagen at Fiskvagnen Linné, a fish stall next to our local supermarket, and the rest of the ingredients from inside the latter. At Systembolaget I bought a sparkling wine that was supposedly a good pairing for seafood, an Italian red for the meat, and a number of IPAs. I can willingly admit that the visit to Systembolaget did stir a certain yearning within me, but by this point I'd been dry for weeks and was completely convinced that I'd literally drown in self-loathing if I had a so-called relapse on a night like this. Especially since I was firmly resolved to seem like a new man! Throwing in the towel and going back to the bottle would be to gamble with that resolve.

The two red glass beads from my Wreath of Christ—the ones known as the Sacrifice bead and the bead of God's Love—reminded me that there is a love that one receives and a love that one offers up. And what I had personally offered up—or *sacrificed*—to be capable of harboring (or offering) a bigger portion of *agape* toward Agnes and Otto was, I reasoned, my outrageous *sense of superiority* vis-à-vis the unhappy couple. Agnes and Otto had failed in the care of their Tamagotchi (Frodo), and this had, as we know, amused the previous version of myself.

Then *I* had failed in the care of my own baby surrogate (Molly), which had forced me to embark upon a journey of discovery within myself. Things that I had regarded as trivial just a few months before—since in my opinion it was mainly "normies" who cared about the things that I, through habit, had viewed as irrelevant—I now regarded (and rated) with new (and perhaps more *normative*) eyes.

As it happens, my religious reillumination was still highly intact by then, perhaps even bolstered by my interest in Jordan B. Peterson—which, I now realize, had been sparked by my dispute with Otto (or in any case Otto's bizarre reaction) at that first dinner. Although I'd finished reading *12 Rules* long ago, I still had a long, long catalog of YouTube lectures left to work through. Apropos Peterson, I certainly had no intention of bringing him up in conversation with Otto again. That was completely out of the question! And I definitely had no intention of driving him insane by reporting on the other fruits of my reading, either.*

Of course, if he should so happen, against the odds, to bring up Peterson again, I would of course have no choice but to say what I really thought; anything else would be cowardice. For obviously I didn't see Peterson as the conservative cryptofascist that Otto had (presumably) thought him at the time of our first meeting. Indeed, if Otto were once again to discuss Peterson in such affected (or *blasphemous*) terms, I would be compelled to confront him, to be sure. I would necessarily have to take to the incomprehensibly misunderstood Peterson's defense, and my argumentation would be to the point, clear and discursive, highly factual, accommodating and understanding, and not at all eager to win at all costs.

"Personally," I would have no choice but to inform Otto, "I actually enjoy Professor Peterson's lectures. In my opinion they are at times extremely interesting—and instructive."

At the same time, I reasoned, should an actual argument about Peterson arise, I would also have to admit that I found

---

*Had it not been for Peterson, there is no guarantee I would have started to read writers like Mircea Eliade, Joseph Campbell, Carl Rogers, and Carl Jung with the same degree of enthusiasm and thirst for knowledge with which I had approached them in recent months.

the man *an exceptionally peculiar person*. Tiresome in his *fragilité*. At times, indeed, perhaps increasingly often, on the verge of tears. A *whiny git*, to put it bluntly. Yes, he was! On top of which, I might also admit that I never quite got Peterson's tendency to equate so-called postmodernism with neo-Marxism. That might perhaps be something that Otto and I could bond over. Since that particular matter (i.e., of equating postmodernism with neo-Marxism) would plausibly be something that would radically provoke Otto, especially since I suspected that he (possibly) saw himself as some sort of Marxist. Indeed, had one been indoctrinated to ascribe an unequivocal value to figures like Derrida and Lacan—and moreover invested time and energy into assimilating their bizarre thinking—it would perhaps be more or less a veritable trauma that a professor of psychology should shoot from the hip, as it were, and out all that for the nonsense it really was.

That being said, I hadn't the slightest intention of bringing up Peterson off my own bat during Agnes and Otto's visit. I had no intention at all of airing topics that seemed to me the slightest bit radioactive, inflammatory, or taboo.

Maria, who still remembered Otto's peculiar Peterson reaction, and how the psychologist, as she put it, seemed to have pretty much "mindfucked" her friend Agnes's partner, sensed the storm cloud hanging over my head just a moment before the potentially problematic guests arrived.

Half in jest, half seriously, she asked if I was planning on "terrorizing" Otto with that Peterson malarkey again. But I guaranteed her that I had truly no intention of doing so, as that would be more or less evil.

For my part, Otto's Peterson reaction had, with time, led to a sort of epiphany. Otto's far-from-anomalous Peterson collapse had spoken to something symptomatic of an entire age, of an increasingly polarized zeitgeist. As though the middle classes were in the throes of a budding collective psychosis.

"Though it's not at all impossible," I reasoned, "that by now Otto's been so exposed to Peterson that he'll be a wonder of stoicism if his name does crop up tonight . . . a bit like in CBT, where they dishabituate people from a phobia of spiders, say."

My—and possibly also, albeit to a lesser extent, Maria's—apprehensions were, as it would turn out, completely unfounded: Peterson's name wasn't mentioned once during Agnes and Otto's visit. Neither at dinner, nor later with coffee (which this time we took at the kitchen table, which was—unusually—topped with a clean and dazzlingly white tablecloth embellished with royal lilies with a silky sheen). I don't believe I myself reflected on Peterson for so much as a single second all night. So, kind of an anticlimax.

Agnes and Otto had turned up around six, just as I was grilling a few slices of pain de mie for my Toast Skagen. The guests exuded good spirits, and it was infectious. Otto had clearly lost weight since we last saw him. Something that Maria wasted no time in pointing out:

"Wow, Otto, you've got so thin!"

I gave a little start, as I feared this would be taken as an insult, but as fate would have it, Otto beamed, after which he revealed that he'd taken up running. It had been such a *breeze* that he was even planning on running the Gothenburg half-marathon in September. *Yes, he really does look healthier,* I thought as I took the bottle of Côtes du Jura that Agnes presented to us as a gift. Indeed, it had been the first thing that had struck me when I'd seen them: *How healthy they look! Really summery.*

The good ambiance boded well.

Just after we'd sat down at the table and kind of delicately started tucking into the starter for which I would later be commended—I had been very careful to follow a Leif Mannerström tip (that I assume I'd read in a book): It was important to (1) keep the prawns' "butter" and (2) add a dollop of Dijon mustard to the mayonnaise and cream; not too much, but just enough to give everything a lift—a minor bomb still went off in my head, when Agnes and Otto informed us that they had just recently become "with cat" again—to a cat, it would emerge, with *special needs.*

Although on this occasion I considered myself a textbook example of propriety—I really didn't lose it! at least not visibly—I still couldn't help but feel an intense anxiety that I would be struck by a case of Tourette's when Agnes pulled out her phone to show us a picture of the new cat. The creature, or, rather, Bubba, as they said it was called, really did look awfully weird. Its eyes pointed in different directions, and its tongue stuck out as though it was too big for the little cat's mouth.

"Bubba has a chromosome abnormality, we think," said Otto.

"You don't say!" I exclaimed enthusiastically—and without any malicious undertone. "You don't say," I said again. "Can cats really have chromosome abnormalities? I had no idea."

"Yes, all animals can have chromosome abnormalities," Otto replied deadpan, but from what I could tell without reading any ill intent into my question.

"Things might not always be so easy going forward," Agnes said, "but he'll still be the *world's cutest Bubba!*" After which she added, a touch laconically: "Though he probably won't live as long as a normal cat."

"But Bubba will still live a *full life* for the years given to him in our care," Otto went on with a dignified air.

Me, I'd been completely unprepared for this bizarre piece of news—I was well and truly floored—but Maria was surprisingly quick on her feet. "Oh, how cute! What heroes you are!" et cetera.

Still, Bubba was pretty cute. Yeah, even I could see that. But I was nonetheless completely gobsmacked that Agnes and Otto had—clearly *knowingly*—gotten a cat who was mentally handicapped.

Agnes told us that a friend's cat had had a litter, and that Bubba had been one of three kittens all born with some kind of disability. After some time had passed and the friend had

realized that Bubba was actually quite okay, Agnes and Otto—
apparently feeling that they had mourned Frodo long enough—
had taken pity on him. The other kittens had, sadly, died after
just a few weeks.

Bubba, on the other hand, had been unusually robust. A
curious and intrepid kitten, Agnes said, a real little mischief-
maker.

I suddenly started to feel an intense need for a time-out,
so I excused myself and went to the toilet for a minute, despite having no call of nature to see to. I just needed to gather
my thoughts for a while. *So they'd gotten themselves a mentally
handicapped cat?*

Yes, they had. Nothing funny about that. Nothing. Funny.
At. All. Obviously I wasn't going to make any cheeky digs.
Humiliating our guests was out of the question! Besides, I reminded myself, Molly was more or less handicapped too. Perhaps I could even make some kind of point of that? I wondered.
She had her odd shaking, for one. But on the other hand, that
had subsided lately. (Indeed, strangely enough, it had basically disappeared since her adventure in the laundry basket.)
No, that was far too risky to touch upon. Best to play it cool.
Despite my self-admonitions, a quote from *Tropic Thunder*
flashed through my head: "Never go full retard." I immediately
repressed it.

After splashing a little cold water on my face, I returned in
time for the main course, which Maria had just served. For a
second I almost reached for the wine bottle, until I remem-

bered I was supposed to stay sober that night. *I've got an ace up my sleeve, at least,* I thought. *Well, why not go on and mention it?* At the table they were still talking about animals with special needs.

"That Grumpy Cat has some sort of syndrome too, no?" I asked cautiously.

It was perfect! Obviously everyone knew who good old Grumpy Cat was! But none of the others knew what type of syndrome it was that made Grumpy Cat quite so *grumpy*. Despite it going against my own rules of etiquette, I fished my mobile out of my pocket and looked up the famous cat on Wikipedia. Yes indeed: Grumpy Cat not only had an underbite, but also, I read aloud, so-called *feline dwarfism*.

"Is that a specific breed of cat?" Maria asked.

"The Munchkin, no?" Otto suggested.

It sounded a little off, I thought, but he was probably completely right—both politically and taxonomically.

Agnes told us about a community that they had found on Instagram, or maybe it was Facebook, for people who were owners of animals that were less fortunate.

"Sadly some people make money from it," said Otto with an outraged, old-fart voice, as though not only meaning to signal that it would be utterly alien to him to do anything of the sort, but also that he considered it a vulgar *faux pas*.

"Don't people sell merch with Grumpy Cat's face on?" I asked.

"No doubt they do!" Otto replied.

Inwardly I argued that it would be difficult to make money off Bubba, to capitalize on him, as it were, as his appearance seemed *generically* retarded, or whatever the right word is. *That probably wouldn't be enough*, I thought. *Obviously you need a USP, too!*

In that particular sense, one could view Grumpy Cat as an exemplary product. For even if there were potentially *Munchkins* galore in this world, there certainly couldn't be so many of them with an underbite to boot, and surely it was largely the latter—perhaps combined with the standoffish gaze—that made Grumpy Cat look so grumpy? Besides, Grumpy Cat had been the first on the ball, as it were.

I put forward my hypothesis that pets like Grumpy Cat and perhaps even Boo—a.k.a *The World's Cutest Dog*—must live pretty fantastic lives, as they were probably extremely well looked after by their owners. The others agreed.

"Boo's a Pomchi just like Molly, right? Only orange?" Maria asked.

"Is Boo still alive?" Agnes asked quizzically. Maria checked Wikipedia . . . and yes, Boo was still going strong.*

There really was a lot of chat about Bubba, Molly, and pets in general over dinner. A few short months before, this would

---

*On the night of this dinner, Boo had only a few months left of this world. He passed away in his sleep in the early hours of the morning on January 18, 2019, at twelve years of age. Tardar Sauce or Grumpy Cat passed away a few months later, in May of the same year. She was seven years old.

probably have driven me to insanity, as I can only assume I would have felt that Agnes and Otto's virtue signaling had reached a veritable apex with the entry of this new pet into their lives. Now, while I obviously found their adoption of Bubba more or less parodic, when all was said and done I could still see that they were genuinely *good people. For reals.* A quality that I had been completely blind to on their first visit. Perhaps mainly because of my own callousness, but also because of Otto's jaw-droppingly intense antipathy toward Peterson. Perhaps I was simply beginning to understand them—as though I was simply *seeing* them for real for the very first time.

Seeing and *accepting* them as they were?

In fact, I couldn't even bring myself to be outraged when Agnes made a fiery little speech in favor of intersectional analysis, even though I could see that *she* basically didn't know what she was on about. I kept completely schtum, listening and observing attentively, neither condemning nor exonerating. Evidently these trendy ideologies were to some degree a *substitute religion.* (That it would all lead to textbook psychosis I didn't yet know at this point, even if I could guess which way the winds were blowing. The term *wokeism* didn't yet enjoy worldwide recognition.) Agnes didn't actually need to know what intersectionality was. (To be fair, who in their right minds actually *got* Trinitarianism?) It made no difference at all. The main thing was, clearly, that she (and Otto) appeared to be good citizens and championed the dogmas of the new Orthodoxy.

That was probably the closest we got to the topic of politics that night, which was just as well. The ambiance stayed pleasant, and I was even surprised at how much more positively I felt about Otto the more he talked about this and that, especially when he impressed me with his educated and unexpectedly profound arguments. For example, Maria mentioned that she had tried to watch the anime classic *Grave of the Fireflies*, which Agnes had recommended at some point, a strikingly dark 1988 film about the firebombings of Japanese wood-built slums at the end of World War II. But Maria had been so overwhelmed by the orphaned siblings' suffering that she had given up just halfway through; I'd had to watch the rest on my own.

Otto said he knew where she was coming from. "Obviously it's a fucking bleak film!" But he also imparted a brilliant analysis that the American film critic Robert Ebert had given of the film:

When the animated film depicts a starving five-year-old girl baking mud balls and chewing on pebbles to dupe her hunger, the stylized animation reveals the very *idea*—the pure *archetype* or more distilled concept—of a starving little girl baking mud balls and chewing on pebbles. In the end she also dies of starvation.

"I mean, it's unbearably sad!" said Otto, and I could only agree.

But in a film that *wasn't* animated, that is, one in which we see a living, breathing little girl do the same thing, Otto said that Ebert had said that we would never read what's depicted as the mere *idea* of a child in grave suffering; we wouldn't tolerate it, it would cut too close to the bone, and as such we viewers would very likely react to it completely differently.

"Now, if it were a 'live action' film, as they call them," Otto speculated, "we would presumably feel such a strong aversion to the suffering depicted, such intense discomfort, that we might not even be able to view the film as art. We wouldn't be shielded by the aesthetic distillation that animation offers."

A, to my ears, staggeringly interesting hypothesis! *The Grave of the Fireflies* would most likely have been completely unbearable were it not for the fact that the animation takes the edge off its extreme realism. Otto developed this argument by drawing parallels to Art Spiegelman's comic *Maus*, which he believed was one of the greatest depictions of the Holocaust in existence, and for roughly the same reasons that made *The Grave of the Fireflies* so special.

"Because the crime against humanity takes a detour, as it were, through the nonhuman, a fable-esque coded, anthropomorphic world of mice and cats," Otto claimed, "the brutal subject is made *manageable*, perhaps so much as digestible. But this animalistic detour is perhaps completely logical in a way," he went on, "since that's how we're socialized as kids. Kids identify with animals, as they're often small and powerless, just like them."

When he uttered these words it seemed as though he'd given himself away, or even revealed too much of his inner world—he did blush a little. Yeah, that makes a lot of sense, I

reasoned, of course—even adults identified with animals generally and cute animals especially; we were powerless to be
anything but *suckers* for the magic of their morphological neo-
teny. Plus there was presumably no end to this so-called socialization. As a matter of fact, adults might even be children, too,
at least that's what Ingmar Bergman—who admittedly wasn't
exactly an *emotional* genius—once said. Adults, according to
that great director, were simply children who *played* at being
adults. The only difference being that they had forgotten that
they were kids.

Despite my complete sobriety, I nevertheless came close to
losing my cool at at least one point during dinner: Maria and
Agnes had gotten into a conversation about the actor Eddie
Redmayne, and I couldn't help but splutter that I didn't get him
or why he was so popular.

"He looks so fucking malnourished!" I said, but the others
very much disagreed.

Agnes put forward his acting chops with strong conviction,
and I capitulated and agreed: Redmayne was certainly a highly
competent actor. But I still couldn't get past the fact that his, in
my view, emaciated physique alarmed me in some way. Instead
of being completely honest, which had been my primary objective, I started to lie and said that Redmayne had been very good
in *The Danish Girl*. A film that I had in fact hated.

Agnes and Otto exhibited no signs of concern whatsoever

at my clear dislike of Redmayne. Or at least they didn't show the slightest semblance of provocation. Perhaps in a way they heard only what they wanted to hear? That or they were far too happy to be troubled by it. Probably thanks to the magnificent, rose-tinted bubble that Bubba's adoption had enveloped them in. Indeed, I was fully taken aback at the harmony they radiated. Or, really, I was especially shocked at how extremely harmonious and robust Otto seemed. The shock of Frodo's disappearance must simply, as I perhaps mentioned earlier—especially four or so months ago—have been much greater than what I myself had realized.

Once we had eaten dessert, made the obligatory comments on the apparently never-ending heat wave, and drank our coffee from our Moomin mugs, Agnes and Otto announced their conspicuously early departure: they were very keen to get back to Bubba. To my great relief they had clearly had a very pleasant time of it. In any case, Otto surprised me by eagerly shaking my hand with *both* of his, like priests usually do—something that definitely hadn't happened the previous time. Anyway, it had felt like a spontaneous expression of genuine appreciation. The dinner had been a success, and I'd managed to remain, I assumed—despite my powerlessness to hide my antipathy toward Eddie Redmayne—largely wholly within the bounds of normativity.

Once Agnes and Otto had left, Maria caught me unawares with a big, long hug in the hall. She smelled good and was clearly extremely content, perhaps also a little tipsy. After a kiss she declared that she was off to take a bath, suggested that I do the dishes and then take Molly out, and finally insinuated—with an indescribable and also quintessentially *Maria* gesture—that *intimacy* was very much in the cards. No arguments here.

The evening had absolutely been an all-out success, and perhaps it was no more than right that it be rounded off in a beautiful way.

As such, I set about my final tasks. Into the bin with the scraps. The prawn shells would have to go out as soon as possible, so I'd take out the bin bags when I went out with Molly.

Rinse the plates, glasses, and cutlery. Everything into the dishwasher. Carefully place a tablet into the dedicated little hatch in the machine. I heard Maria laugh in the bath and assumed she was listening to a podcast or similar. Once I was finished with the dishes, I looked around for a while for the pink lead, the restless dog at my heels. When I found it, I was just making to hook it onto her collar when I got caught, as was my habit, in front of my reflection in the full-length mirror. Unlike the last time Agnes and Otto had been over, this time I felt no alienation whatsoever from what I saw before me. Perhaps I did look a little drained, but above all I thought I looked very satisfied. I'd had a genuinely nice time—and on top of that without drinking anything but fizzy water (something the guests barely commented on at all). I stood up straight, reflexively pinched the subcutaneous fat on my belly, and chuckled to myself. It had been some exaggeration on my part to think

I had a so-called *dad bod*. Definitely not! But, sure, obviously I wasn't in my twenties anymore. That was how it was. The cashier at Systembolaget hadn't asked me for ID, either. So my exterior at least gave the impression of belonging to an adult, even if all things considered I was perhaps only simulating that adulthood.

It suddenly hit me that I was probably a very privileged person. A *de facto* privileged person. Anyway, I felt . . . well, *lucky*. At the end of the day, didn't I basically have most of what I needed in life?

A pretty okay job. Yes, it really was. Plus my salary had gone up by a few thousand. And I was in good physical and (I assume) mental health. *Mens sana in corpore sano.* I had, perhaps, dabbled in real alcoholism over that long, hot summer; my retrograde romanticization of alcohol and drugs had, so to say, led me to a *brush* with real dependency. Yes, that was probably true. It might not have been quite as serious as I'd imagined, but serious enough that a long period of teetotalism was still thoroughly justified.

I had Maria, too—Maria with her androgynous, silver-elf look, at times fairer than the sun itself—and she was obviously great—she proved that to me time and time again! Perhaps she was even more great than I deserved?

The thought should move me, I told myself. Molly was a big part of my life now, in a much more profound way than before (because I almost killed her?), and I pretty much took that as a godsend.

She was no mere surrogate, Molly, but a unique little creature, with her own little feelings, thoughts, and behaviors. (Indeed, according to Ramakrishna's beliefs, one could go so far as to say that she, like myself, was an aspect or manifestation of God!) Besides these two, my very nearest and dearest, I also had educated friends and acquaintances (a circle that, with time, could perhaps even number Otto, the historian of ideas?).

Claes, my manager at the Unit, had recently lent me Nick Bostrom's *Superintelligence: Paths, Dangers, Strategies*, which I was reading with great interest. Together with Johannes and a mutual acquaintance I had set up a book group that planned to tackle all of Proust's *In Search of Lost Time*. Seven parts. Thousands of pages. An ambitious and optimistic project.

There were yet more grains of gold in my petty bourgeois existence. There were reasons to be grateful! For my sobriety. For its *predictability*. That my life would still continue to consist of (quote) *a bunch of vague anxieties that are never really resolved* (unquote) was something that I would unquestionably have to accept. For my mostly undramatic existence could never resemble the clearly delineated classical drama, with its progressive plot, emotional climax, and resolution. Perhaps I would never, ever be able to understand the classical Aristotelian dramaturgical model. But was it possible, I argued, that none of that really mattered?

Since perhaps no one—not one person!—actually understood all that anymore?

A both pleasing and comforting hypothesis.

That I was incapable of writing a sound story, from A to Z, was something that I would get over eventually. My dream of writing was probably just a sort of . . . hysteria or something. What had actually appealed to me about writing from the start? Status? Possibly. But even my white-collar role possessed a sort of value, too, no? Duty, honor.

Being a real writer would probably, I rationalized with myself, mean far too uncertain an existence, at least in the long term.

Nor would I ever, I thought, as I finally hooked the lead onto Molly's collar, succeed in being a Houellebecq or a seriously significant *readable* writer. For I had no desire to pay the price; I was keen to keep my teeth as long as possible. Nor did I have the slightest inclination to become one of the half-educated "dregs" at the bottom of the literary hierarchy, to use one of Johannes's terms. That was for other idiots to do. Nor could I stoop to writing fucking *Scandi noir*. Completely unthinkable. As such, I reasoned, I should give up my dream of ever writing a novel. Shut that down. Bury it. All of it. The whole shebang.

Indeed, could it not be the case, I thought as I took the lift downstairs, that my so-called dream of writerhood had just been a flight of fancy, from reality, responsibility, love? Peterson was probably right. Life might well be pure suffering and an essentially hopeless struggle, but its meaning was nevertheless: love.

That the Time of Reality was over, that the West was heading toward its downfall, perhaps didn't really mean all that much in the end. Its degeneration had long since been a fact. Nor would I ever get away from the fact that I had *a postmodern brain*.

After all, everyone did nowadays! At least according to Johannes.

But natural and/or sexual selection would eventually reward the race that could survive in a *milieu* that had increasingly come to be characterized by depersonalization-derealization disorder. A secondary reality! A mass psychosis!

Perhaps it didn't even matter if humanity (as Bostrom posited) lived in a computer simulation or not: not so long as one followed society's moral codes, internalized an acceptable persona, and did one's best to fit in. Cleaning one's room was a good start.

7.01